MOTHERLAND

By

Dwight D. Turner

To my lovely wife;
for being all that a partner, friend and lover could be,
and so so much more.

PART ONE

One

The words he used were vile, this man my father, calling that woman my mother a cunt, a whore, a bitch: all this to the woman he'd been married to for over thirty years, that woman he once proclaimed to love.

In retaliation, my mother met his bile with her own, calling him a bastard, a thief, and an impotent old man: brandishing her own words of hate at this man she had once dedicated herself to in a house of god.

He threw hot tea at her, scalding her, blistering her elderly brown self, leaving patches of her bare skin hanging free, revealing the pure white snow beneath.

Without crying out, without saying a word my mother crawled across the floor to her dressing table, before pulling herself up so she could see herself in the mirror. There she stared at herself, seeing in the glass her own shock, her pain reflected back to her as those patches of herself hung limp like unglued wallpaper.

In that same mirror image she saw the bedroom behind her, and watched as her husband then launch himself, his face a mask of uncontained rage. He grabbed her by that table, pushing her forward before spinning her around, grabbing her by the throat before raining down blow after jagged, painful blow.

His force was that of a lion, the accuracy that of a hunter, whilst my mother screamed and tried to defend herself, tried to fight back, tried to meet her husband's fire with her own, tried to face his rage with her hands raised, claws scratching at his white haired head as she brought forward her defence.

Then she fell to the floor, and his feet kicked out at her, like a footballer practicing his free kicks, his craft, striking the ball again and again, almost methodical in his accuracy.

It was then she began to scream, that my mother began crying out, pleading for her life, begging for the beating to stop, for this torment of her to cease, this brutalisation to end.

And when after what must have been an age it ended, when he finally became exhausted with his own aggression, when that man my father stopped and saw what he had done, he just left her there on that floor, in that bedroom with the wallpaper dating back to the seventies. My father, that man, just went back to bed to read the rest of his paper, leaving my mother, that woman, to gather herself, torn clothes, beaten face, blistering skin and all, to crawl out of that bedroom.

When she called me at work, I knew right then that everything I understood of my family had ended, that everything had changed.

I just had no idea how much.

"Karl!" From the moment I picked up the phone at work and heard her voice, I knew it was serious.

"What's wrong mother?"

"I need you to sort out your father!" she said stammering through her sobbing, fighting with her evident anger. "He just threw a cup of hot coffee at me and then started hitting me!"

I heard my father's voice behind her, his footsteps as he came up the stairs. "Stay out of it!" His words, were they for me?

My mother turned to him. "You know what? You're sick! Sick in the head! I'm going to call the police on you this time!"

"This time?" I said, finally finding my voice, surprised as I was.

"Go on then!" my father shouted. I could imagine his thin, elderly frame still towering over her, still threatening. This was my father, this was the man of the house as I remembered him, and even though he was still older than my mother by nearly a decade he still carried himself with authority, and often also with menace.

"You know what they will do if I call them!"

"Well, do it!" he shouted in retaliation. Then I heard him stalk off down the hallway, probably towards the bathroom.

My mother turned to talk to me on the phone. "What should I do Karl, tell me! Do I call the police?"

I could feel a part of me resist getting involved, a part of me that wanted to leave them both to it, to run away from that phone right then and deny them my aid. Was it my place to interrupt the fights between two elderly people, even if they were my parents? Was is my role to referee their disagreements? I had no answers for myself.

"How badly injured are you?" I asked, my voice as calm as I could manage.

"My skin, oh my skin," she said softly, painfully. "I need to see someone. And my head is sore."

"Do you need to go to the hospital?"

"I don't know. If I don't then I don't know if my head will be all right, and if I do then they will come and arrest him. You know that don't you?"

"Yes mother?"

"But what if I have a blood clot? What if I suffer from a brain haemorrhage and die? Then you can tell them what happened can't you?"

I sat there, aching with that pull in both directions. This wasn't my problem, I had my own life to take care of, I didn't need this right now, not with the fight I'd had with Lilly last night. I had things to do, work to complete before my holiday, and didn't want my parents causing me problems. For some strange reason I was torn, pulled in two by the most obvious of decisions. Your mother is in pain, help her.

Yet for some reason I didn't want to. I didn't want to be her knight, her hero, her saviour. Again.

There was a long pause on the phone.

"Karl?"

"I think you have to do what you feel is best mum. I can't solve this problem for you."

As I said the words I could almost feel the sadness come back to me down the phone line, and then felt my own guilt rise because of it. I could have killed myself in that second. She needed me. She needed me to save her, to protect her from my father right then, and I had just refused her. I had just stopped myself from doing the obvious thing: being the defender, sacrificing myself at the feet of my own father to prolong the life of my mother.

It was scary just how much I could feel of this woman, my mother, this seventy-odd-year-old as she grimaced, though didn't know if it was from the pain of her injuries alone. "I think I should go to the hospital," she whispered.

"I will take you," I replied reluctantly.

It was discovering the abuse that finally prompted me to leave.

The tales that tormented me once I learned about them left me not knowing who I was anymore, or where I was going.

I don't know how long we we're in the hospital, but once they heard about what had been going on at home, once we all saw the extent of my mother's injuries, the doctors and nurses were obliged to call in the police. She looked as bad as I thought she would, her skin hanging free and almost flapping when she spoke like she were some kind of Heron or other bird: the rest of her face a mask of bruises and blisters, her left eye almost closed.

Then, when a couple of officers, one male and one female, finally arrived, and started taking a statement from my mother, the whole story came out. For nearly forty years this had been going on, the systematic mistreatment of a woman by a man, of my mother by my father.

From the recent emotional abuse of the mischief calls he had made to her friends, to her family, and to her work, to the days on end when he would ignore her, when he would readily leave the room when she walked in, and not relate to her for the smallest indiscretion.

Or the occasional black eyes I barely used to see in my twenties and teens when I still just about lived at home. Those irregular morning results from the arguments the night before: those whispered voices that grew and grew. Voices that became firm, became angry, became so loud that they would erupt into snap flashes of aggression, then be over in an instant. They more often occurred, she said, when I was away from the house and out with either friends or girlfriends.

Then there were the times when I was a child when I would see him shouting at her, berating her for something she had done or not, with the occasional slap thrown in for good measure. Or those times I was too young to remember, like the one my mother told the police about, when he threw a potty of piss at her in the middle of the night as she had gotten up to comfort my fussing self in my cot.

More and more stories she told the two policemen, going further and further back through our history as a family, dredging up shame, guilt and anger. These tales sliding all the way back to when he beat her, with an anger comparable to today, when my father punched her in the stomach, the face, the groin: back then she was a woman three months pregnant with myself.

For nearly two hours my mother told the policemen all of this. These horrific stories going back to before I was even born, during her pregnancy with me, and during the early years of my life there had been arguments, beatings, abuse, rapes, kicking, biting, bruising, tripping, and her life had been a hell on earth.

The shock prompted me to recall my own times when I still lived in that house: a thirty-nine year old black man, sitting in a hospital whilst looking back on a childhood and parents he had always thought of as normal, yet only then realising that it was nothing of the sort at all. With a mother who would control, manipulate and beat me when she was in one of her moods, and a father who would do the same and more: who would undermine, blame and sabotage, and whom I felt always hated me.

The police took photographs, and asked me what I knew of today, which was not much I told them: I wasn't there after all and my guilt about that was huge. Then, they accompanied us back home and said they would arrest my father, and would be taking him to a police station so they could interview him.

As I stood outside my parent's home in the cold hour just before midnight, and watched my father being taken to a waiting police car, I felt an immense amount of guilt and shame: guilt that I had failed to protect my mother, and the shame of having to witness my own elderly father being arrested.

I stayed with my mother that night. Her protector making sure the doors were locked and we were safe. Then I went to bed, but I couldn't sleep, I just lay there tossing and turning, thoughts running through my head about why I'd frozen. Why had I decided not to take a stand and protect my mother from my father? Why hadn't I done my duty?

That night I had a dream that:

I was a superhero. And the world was once more in danger, this time from mechanical men who wanted to take over the planet and enslave its population. They had come to the Earth in huge triangular ships, ships that would hover over largely populated areas and systematically destroy them. From my hideout, within an ancient temple hidden in the Amazon jungle, I feel them, or rather the planet does, before Mother Earth rouses me from my slumber, and bids me to do her bidding.

So I fly to them. I rise up into the sky and fly to these ships, and I destroy them. Using heat from my eyes, the cry of my voice, and the strength of my bare hands I melt, shatter, and break them. I fly around the planet and defeat them, sending any that escape to flee up into the skies once more.

When I've won though, the heads of state want to honour me, but they decide that they can't.

"But why?" asks a young boy in a small town in America.

"Because we don't know who he is," replies the United Nations Attorney General.

And then it strikes me. This is all I am. I have no alter ego. I have no other life other than this one. For the first time I'm aware that I don't have the job of a Clark Kent or a Peter Parker, and I'm not a millionaire like Bruce Wayne or a Tony Stark.

I am nothing beyond my superhero.

I am nothing.

"Mum?" I said as I approached my mother in the kitchen a few days later. She was washing some dishes, and as she turned to me I could see her eyes were still bloodshot. I doubted she'd gotten much sleep since father had been barred from the house. "I have to tell you something."

In the week since, our lives had been difficult but we had managed. My father had been banned from the house following his being bailed to return the day after his arrest, and seemed to be keeping a low profile. He had strangely denied any wrongdoing, even with all the evidence to the contrary, so the police had decided to charge him. Following a brief appearance in the local Magistrates Court the next morning it was made a condition of his bail that he not have any contact with my mother and not return home.

I didn't go to court to see him: I couldn't as I was still completing all that work I had left over. In addition, it wasn't as if my father had even bothered to contact me, his son, I guess out of shame, or out of pride, and that I found particularly odd, yet also totally normal.

Mother though had been keeping herself busy. She had not told anyone about what had happened to her, and was spending a lot of time at home, but at least she was on the mend. Her skin would heal, and she had been given oils and salves to aid its progress, but she was still occasionally in a lot of pain. The bruises on her face had started to go down, but at their height they were really quite horrible to witness. I had no idea how she was coping with the emotional toll from everything that had taken place, that had split my family apart, and she had chosen not to talk to me about it.

These days though had left me feeling the strain, the tension that came with trying to hold another's pain, and her silence was starting to get to me. After a number of days I knew I needed a break.

"Remember that holiday I told you about?" I continued.

Mother stopped what she was doing and turned towards me. I could see her eyes were already filling with water.

"Well, I'm still going. I'm flying to Africa this weekend."

"What?"

"Because I need to get a away for a couple of weeks. I need a rest from everything."

I could see the pleading in her eyes. "But I need you here."

"I need to get away mum. Please, it will only be for a short while. Your sisters and friends will help I'm sure if you let them, and if you speak to your Pastor then I know the church will support you as well."

My mother seemed unconvinced. "I don't think I can manage without you."

"You will be fine. I promise I will only be gone a couple of weeks."

"Alright." I could hear and feel the choked sound in her voice.

It almost broke my heart to witness it, and the guilt rising was painful, so incredibly painful.

So nearly two weeks after my father almost put my mother in hospital, and with a heavy, guilt-ridden heart, I took myself off for a safari holiday in Zambia.

Two

This trip was supposed to be the one where I relaxed, and simply recovered from the stress of life. Now though, it was a thinly disguised chance to run away from my family, to escape the horrors being shown to me in all their glory. I was therefore relieved when the day finally arrived and I travelled out to Heathrow Airport.

When Busta turned up late as usual to drive me to the airport I didn't fret, I just kept on whistling some nameless tune in my head from the night before, distracting myself from my guilt. After he'd dropped me off, I acted happy as I stood there at the winding Check-In queue. I pretended to be cheerful as they asked me to take off my belt and shoes and place the in one of the baskets so they could be scanned, and was even still fake-smiling when informed that my flight to Johannesburg with South African Airways would be delayed by two hours.

I allowed myself to pretend that I didn't care about all of the hassles of leaving the West. That all I was worried about was my first trip to the Motherland.

Africa.

"Why go there?" my friends had asked me collectively when I told them.

These were questions I constantly asked myself as I planned my trip, queries that countered everything I had ever thought about the Dark Continent, as it was once called.

For example, when I was a kid no one wanted to go to Africa. It must be a horrible place, my childhood peers and I would say: full of disease and poverty, riddled with corruption and revolution, with no history, no heroes, no past worth speaking of, just the images of Tarzan serials and old movies. We even used to call each other 'an African' when we thought the other was stupid, mirroring how they were so often portrayed. The only things that sold it to me as I became older were the wonderful pictures of the wildlife: the words of Attenborough, the pictures of the BBC, the World Music, the sensitive stories that occasionally crossed my path and touched me.

I wanted to experience some of this on this break, to take myself away and dip my feet in a pool I had been so afraid of when I was a child.

Now though, I understood my recent dream had disturbed me, but that wasn't the first time I'd had an experience like that one, the only time something had hinted that something wasn't right within me.

Yet I didn't understand why. I thought I was happy. My job working for a Mental Health Charity had served me well for five years, even if it was demoralising. Nothing ever changed in mental health: the wards were still as white walled and the cells as padded as they had been in the days when the gentry would pay a penny to see the mad people perform. The rules were still as antiquated when I began the job, and the Service Users were still as unwilling to take charge and change things for themselves. It was a demoralising job, a thankless task in a thoughtless system for a powerless people, and I was beginning to resent the lot of them.

Personally, I had only recently left home, finding a room upstairs in the loft of a house just a couple of streets away from my parent's place in Harlesden. I rented, I lived on my own, but I still regularly ventured home, my mother still cooked many of my meals, and I still often brought washing for her to do.

I had a very active social life. I dated not one but two women: Sally, Swedish, working in PR, saw me from time to time when she wasn't busy running around the country. Our way of relating involved regular great sex and occasional adequate dinners, often in that order. Then there was Lilly, a homely Afro-Caribbean girl, who worked alongside me, and was the single mother of a troubled boy nearing double figures in age. Ours was an odd relationship. Although we spent a fair amount of time together it never seemed as if we were going to develop in to anything serious.

I didn't get anything more useful than that from them really, yet they were still large parts of my life. When I felt low, I might occasionally talk to them about how I was feeling, but I never received any advice of any use to me. I once even spent several weeks seeing a counsellor, a woman who just asked me a lot of questions about my childhood, before asking me to visualise where I might like my life to go five years from now. All I managed to 'visualise' was my boot going up her backside, but I couldn't tell her that, so I never went back.

It was when the difficulties were at their height on a day I learnt of yet another funding cut might threaten my position in mental health, just a month before that call from my mother, that I knew I needed a break. I had seen an advert in the Sunday papers just that week, offering organised tours of Zambia: Safari, relaxation, that kind of thing, and I immediately felt drawn to it.

"Travel through the lush game reserves that border the Zambezi: visit the majesty that is Victoria Falls!" it read excitedly.

Cutting it out from the Travel Section I pinned it on my wall at home, along with all the other scraps of paper I never used again, hoping that this one might actually be of benefit to me.

Buying myself the last ticket for the trip, and being forced into also obtaining an Open Return flight ticket, as there were no others available, I travelled to seek out that benefit.

After a long but relaxed flight, I just made my connection onwards to Lusaka, the hour in Johannesburg one of the most challenging of my life, but even that didn't dampen my mood. And when I finally arrived in Zambia and stepped out of the air-conditioned airplane, onto the steps, and finally down onto the warm tarmac, I wanted to cry.

I was here at last.

I was free from my home.

After collecting my luggage and clearing customs, I pushed my trolley out into the throng of the airport, feeling myself immediately assaulted by the heat of the day, and the heat of the black faces before me, of the people all demanding something from me.

"Can I help you with your luggage boss?"

"Where are you going boss? Do you want a taxi?"

"Do you need to change any money boss?"

"No thank you," I replied as politely as possible, looking about furiously, scanning the crowd for my Tour Leader, suddenly nervous at all of the attention I seem to be receiving.

"Are you sure boss?" someone asked.

I ignored him as I finally saw what I was looking for: my name, Karl Taylor, on a large board held by thin white arms, high above someone's head. I quickly ambled made my way through the crowd towards it.

"I'm Karl Taylor."

The attractive young woman seemed momentarily surprised, but then quickly recovered her composure, giving me her hand to shake. "Welcome to Zambia, Mr Taylor," she said in accented English, almost shouting above the noise of the mainly men talking all around us. "I'm Ilse, your Guide for the next two weeks. I see you didn't arrive too late in the end. Did you have a good trip?"

"Yes thanks," I replied. "And please call me Karl."

"Thank you Karl. The others are all in the minibus. They haven't been waiting for too long, but I think we should join them as you are the last one to arrive."

"Oh, am I? I'm sorry."

"Don't be," Ilse added, before confidently guiding me through the throng and towards the exit. "There are always delays here in Zambia, in fact across Africa. We try to build leave enough time into the schedule so that they don't disturb our tours too much."

As I watched her, I realised I could feel she was an experienced traveller, so I followed her as we exited out into the hot and humid air. Looking around, I trailed behind Ilse as she meandered towards a large bus with several people already sitting inside, patiently waiting.

Ilse waved and shouted something in a language I didn't understand, prompting an African man to exit from the bus, and walk towards us, leaning forward to grasp my bag before I ask him.

"Thank you," I said to him politely.

The man looked up at me and nodded twice, before opening up the trunk and pushing my bag inside with all the others.

"If you could climb onboard Karl."

"Sure."

A sea of different faces greeted me as I walked into the cooler air-conditioned air, some male, some female, all white. As I walked down the aisle I immediately noticed that it was the younger ones who said hello to me. The older ones seemed a bit stiff and distant, a bit unsure of me perhaps, leaving me with a feeling I thought I'd left behind in London, an ugly feeling that raised an anxiety in my stomach.

I sat down quietly: suddenly feeling exhausted, blaming it on the length of my journey, as the bus pulled away from the airport.

And there was I, with six other people, all very different, all my companions on this trip of my lifetime, as we headed away to our hotel for our first night together.

I deny the obvious fact that, besides the driver, I'm the only black person here.

"What made you come to Africa?" one of the American girls asked me later over dinner.

"Well, I've always wanted to go on safari," I replied blandly. "I've been to Asia and America, and done most of Europe, so I thought Zambia was next."

"Oh cool, where about did you go to in Asia?" she continued excitedly.

"Well, I've been to Bangkok a couple of times…"

"Oh yes, crazy place." This time, when she spoke she was so excited that she didn't realise she had just interrupted me.

"True. I could only stand it for a couple of days at a time. Too humid for me, though the people are good fun."

"Where else did you go in Thailand?"

"Well, when I was last there, which was quite a while ago, I went to Ko Samui, and…"

"Yeah, yeah, and did you go to the Full Moon Party?" And again.

"No, not that time. I was there more to relax than anything."

"You should do it sometime. It's really cool. Tanya and myself met some really great Australian guys there last time. We got so fucked up together. All the drugs and drink. When we've done this trip we're going out to Brisbane to meet them."

"Good for you," I replied, nodding my head and smiling politely.

The place we stayed at for our first day in Lusaka was a guesthouse on the outskirts of town, a small, self-contained place, behind high walls with crushed glass and barbed wire and guards. Even with these military style additions, the hotel had its own restaurant, a bar, and a large television, that on that first evening screened an English football match being played live back home.

The place was quiet and the rooms were functional but comfortable, all with en-suite bathrooms, clean white towels, a television, and tea and coffee making facilities, everything an Englishman man might need on his first visit to Africa.

It was late afternoon by the time we arrived at the guesthouse, and nearly time for dinner, so Ilse encouraged us all to take an hour to unpack and freshen up a little, before meeting back at the bar for an evening drink, dinner, and a chance to meet and greet each other properly.

So there I was, seated at one of several plastic tables that had been pushed together to make a longer one, next to two American girls: Tanya from a small place out in Colorado, and Robin from Brooklyn, New York. They were students at NYC, and it was Robin who was firing questions at me about my travels, whilst simultaneously answering them herself.

The Americans were the only two who were younger than me I also found out, as along the table to my right were a couple from Kent: Hazel was English and Marco was Scottish. He had been an officer in the Royal Air Force for a number of years, was even based in Berlin at the time with the Berlin Wall finally fell, Hazel had told me earlier during the meal. Following their return from Germany he then left the military and worked in the City in London for several years, making a lot of money it appeared. On the back of this, and with their two children now departed and settled down in their own lives, they had both taken early retirement, and to celebrate he'd taken his wife away on a series of trips around the world.

"This is our third trip," Hazel continued, in a break from the narcissistic grilling the American was giving me. "We've already visited Antarctica on a cruise ship from Chile, and travelled across New Zealand in a Campervan. Next up Marco wants for us to drive across Canada, and then maybe spend some time travelling through Eastern Europe, isn't that right darling?"

Marco just 'humphed' as if he was already bored by the subject.

Opposite me, the other pair were Randal and Kerry from South Africa, who were a blonde haired, suntanned, married couple in their mid-forties, and were on their third holiday to Zambia.

They were pleasant enough in greeting me, but didn't have much to say. Randal seemed more interested in chatting to Tanya, his eyes regularly drifting down to her cleavage. The American though seemed bored by whatever he had to say to her and kept pushing her food around her place, whilst also nervously watching the waitresses who busily attended to us as we ate our evening meal.

"Can I get you another drink sir?" one of the ladies said to me over my shoulder.

"Er, no thank you," I replied, a little uncomfortable at being called a sir.

"Well, I will have another drink, if you don't mind," Randal added, waving his glass in the waitress' direction.

"Of course," she replied, quickly moving around the table to attend to him.

"And what about you?" asked Robin, finally choosing to make conversation. "What do you do back at home?"

"Well," I replied. "I work for mental health survivors group of men and women from the BME Communities."

"BME?" Hazel asked.

"Black and Multi Ethnic."

"What does that mean?" Randal snorts.

"Well it means anyone from the Black, Asian and other communities. It's a group for those who feel disadvantaged within the mental health system back at home."

"So, do you have mental health problems as well?" Hazel asked, perhaps a little too quickly.

I smiled at her as reassuringly as I could. "No, I just work for them. I help coordinate their campaigns, set up their weekly meetings, and arrange trips to visit other organisations around Britain and worldwide."

"Sounds interesting," Robin added.

"It used to be," I replied.

The conversation soon moved on to why everyone was there on this particular trip. Besides the two couples that were on holiday, the American girls were in Africa as a taster before deciding if they wanted to do any voluntary work out here in the future. I gave only the blandest reasons for why I was there, not wanting to tell them the truth: to embarrass myself by confessing that I had left home to escape the horror of my parents marriage break-up. Why make them feel uncomfortable, I convinced myself.

"I'm just here on holiday as I need a rest from London life."

"Oh yes," Hazel added. "Marco always talks about how he hates London. He misses Scotland, yet still prefers the heat and sunshine. He can't stand it when its wintertime at home. He gets very depressed."

At that point, Marco locked eyes with me for the first time, but said nothing, before slowly turning away, his attention artificially elsewhere.

At the end of the meal, Ilse, who had been out for a couple of hours but didn't say where, came by and informed us that this first evening was free but we would have an orientation meeting in the morning after breakfast before doing a couple of excursions should we wish to.

Randal then invited Marco to have a drink with him and his wife, whilst Hazel excused herself and retired to her room. The two Americans then decided to go out and find a bar or club to spend some time with, leaving me uninvited by anyone, and unsure of where to place myself in this group.

"Hmmm."

"Not sure what to do?" Ilse asked coming over to me.

"No, although I am a bit tired, so I might have an early night."

"Well, if you feel like it, I know of a good club we could go to tomorrow evening after dinner. Might be nice to get out and see some of the nightlife here in Lusaka whilst you still can."

I found myself brightening up a little. "Thanks, that could be fun."

"Good, I will see you in the morning."

Later, as I lay under my mosquito net, I found I couldn't sleep, so just lay there with the sound of the crickets somewhere, and the humming of the occasional irritating mosquito, keeping me awake.

Something was bothering me about that evening, about why I'd chosen not to tell the rest of the group about my reasons for coming to Africa. They didn't need to know about my family, about the distress at home, the life I was leaving behind, but I could have been more honest about my own motivations, couldn't I?

Yet, what would they know about feeling lost in the world, I asked myself. They all seemed like people who understood themselves, who knew their places in society. They were all white, all from areas of the world where black people were considered less than them. From America, to Europe, to South Africa, the history of black people was always one of being under or subservient to those of other colours.

Or was that just my vision of them? Was it easier to see them this way as it gave them an authority that I didn't believe I deserved? Was I less than, because I believed I was less than? And actually I was just the same as everyone else.

With thoughts like these starting to permeate it took a while to finally fall off to sleep at the end of my first day in the Motherland.

Three

"This morning, we will be taking the scheduled trip out to the Kabwata Cultural Centre," Ilse had said, speaking in a loud, semi-authoritative voice as we all settled down on the bus. "We will probably spend a couple of hours there, before returning here for lunch. Then this afternoon there is the chance to visit the National Museum. Just to remind you, the trip this afternoon is optional, so if there are any of you who are maybe still feeling the affects of jetlag please do not feel obliged to come along."

"If I wanted to go to museums then I could have done that in London," Marco mumbled. Turning slightly, I just caught Hazel elbowing him in the side in an attempt to quiet him.

The morning was a bright one, and the weather warm but with a nice cooling breeze as the bus pulled away from the hotel and my group took its first excursion together in Zambia.

Still feeling tired, and after a night of broken sleep, I decided not to pay too much attention to anyone else on the bus, preferring instead to sit near the back, and just gaze out of the window at the irregular traffic on a mid-morning in Lusaka.

Coming to a traffic light the bus stopped, and a man walked past, wearing a white shirt and slacks, and holding a series of items, including a tall lamp and shade. On seeing a bus full of people he then started gesturing towards us excitedly.

"Whatever does he want?" asked Hazel, looking across the bus.

"They're for sale," Robin replied. "They all do it. For some of them it's the only way to make any money at all."

"Who in the world is going to stop and buy a lampshade out here?" laughed Marco looking across at Randal who snorted his agreement.

The lights then changed, and as the bus pulled away I glanced back at the man on the pavement, his wares for sale draped all over his body, and found myself secretly marvelling at his ingenuity.

Eventually, we arrived at the Cultural Centre and disembarked into a dusty area with dozens of huts and a number of other buildings set behind them.

I smiled to myself as the occupants of the huts came out to greet us: salesmen, working for the day, immediately starting their pitch in an attempt to encourage us to buy something.

"No thank you!" said Marco sharply to one particular man who hadn't actually said anything, but had shown the temerity to come directly up to him holding a couple of wooden elephants.

The man backed off immediately, looking a little shocked.

"Don't be so mean," Hazel countered, slapping him on the arm, and making Marco jump.

The man retreated to his hut talking furiously in a language none of us recognise, so Hazel followed him, making an all too obvious attempt to smooth any ruffled feathers left by that brief interchange.

"We have up until 12.30pm here, so make the most of the time," ordered Ilse, that ever-present thin smile on still her lips.

"Come on. Let's go and check out some of the stalls over there," said Robin excitedly, pointing out several huts positioned far enough away from the entrance to the Centre to not be very busy at the moment. Tanya shrugged in her usual way and followed her eager friend.

I walked a way behind them, not wanting to be left stuck with the Brit and the Scot, and feeling increasingly uncomfortable in the presence of the South African couple, although I didn't really understand why.

Catching up with the two women, I noticed that they had quickly engaged several young Zambian men, and were energetically discussing which of the statues or bracelets would suit them best.

I continued ambling past them a short way, spotting a man who was busy with a hammer and a small chisel, sculpting away at a large piece of wood.

Standing beside him, he ignored me as I watched him for a while, studying this man below me on the ground, seated with a elephant taking shape out of the ill formed piece of timber.

The man stopped and looked up at me. "Can I help you sir?"

Suddenly realising I was staring I looked a little startled. "Oh, I'm sorry. I didn't mean to do that. I was just fascinated by what you were doing. I hope you don't mind."

"No, sir, that is alright." He looked at me curiously. "Where are you from?"

"I'm from London," I replied.

The man nodded his head to me. "My name is Matthew. Would you like to try?"

A wave of British reserve suddenly hit me. "I don't know if I should."

Then Matthew held up his tools to me, not wanting to take no for an answer. "Please. It will be my pleasure to show you."

I hesitated at that moment, feeling a shyness that I didn't really recognise. As I looked at Matthew, who was still smiling at me curiously, I found myself compelled to give this thing, this carving a go. So, taking the tools I sat down next to him. "What do I do?"

Matthew then spent several minutes showing me the best way to hold the hammer and chisel, before he sat back and let me have a go on my own. I was tentative at first, softly hammering away, and letting the chisel slip along the wood, but soon I got the hang of it, scooping the stray pieces of wood away without making too much of a mess.

Away from the others, I found myself becoming lost right there; lost in the art of my making, next to this man who was just watching me. And each time I glanced up at him, he just nodded to me to continue.

Looking back I was surprised by how comfortable I was in his presence.

"Hey! Karl is making a donkey!"

Reality snapped back into focus. Looking up I spotted Marco shouting across the dusty earth towards the others, several of whom turned to find out what all the fuss was about. I noticed Randal pointing over in my direction, a broad smile on his face.

"He's gone native already!" Marco continued, laughing at his own joke.

Hesitating, I quickly put down the tools, thanking Matthew for his time and patience.

"My pleasure," he replied. "Would you like to buy anything?"

"No," I answered, a little more sharp than I intended. "No, thank you. Maybe next time."

Matthew then shrugged at me and went back to his work, leaving me between him and the others, stranded between cultures.

As I walked back to the others, Kerry came over to me, smiling gently.

"Didn't find anything you wanted to buy?" she asked. Given my initial impression of her wasn't that positive, she seemed to deliver her words with more kindness than I expected.

I shook my head in reply.

"Maybe next time."

"Maybe," I added, before I climbed back onto the bus and waited for the others to return.

Only the two couples went out to the National Museum during the afternoon: the South Africans as they were probably the least jetlagged of us all, and Hazel and Marco because she wanted to, and he had no choice in the matter.

Tanya and Robin stayed behind as they wanted to go for a walk in the city on their own: to explore and do the things that young people liked to do, but they did say they would be back well before dinnertime as Ilse had promised to take them to a nightclub that evening as well.

As for myself, I stayed in the bar, drinking a local beer whilst watching the British football repeated from the evening before on satellite television. Then, when I realised how stupid it was to come all this way only to do something I could normally do at home anyway, I went and checked my email on the computers situated next door.

There was a messaged from my mother, sending me her love, and telling me how much she missed having me around. I could have smiled, or felt some sense of live, but her message just left me feeling guilty and angry ire at her and I didn't understand why. Why was I so angry? And why was I so guilty about being angry with her?

After sitting there for a good while, I decided not to reply to her email, closing it abruptly, and choose as to try as hard as I could to blank it from my memory, realising that I don't want her intruding on my trip. This is my time away, my time to search for myself, my time to recover from the trauma I've been through.

"I can't rescue her anymore," I found myself whispering.

The guilt hit me almost as soon as the words exit my mouth.

Then I read another email, this time from Sally email, telling me she'd bought something fun and sexy and teasing me into guessing what it might be. I smiled at her cheek, remembering just how free and passionate the nights we'd been together had been. If anything she was the only person I regretted not spending time with before I left, so I send her a reply. Still smiling to myself, I write telling her that I've gone away, and won't be around to meet her this weekend. I don't tell her where I've gone, or why, but I do say that I am well and having a good time. I also suggest that she keeps the surprise for another time, and promise her that we will have fun with it when I return.

Lastly, I sit back and leaf through the various articles from the online paper I subscribe to, scanning an article about the group of people from Harlesden who travelled to the coast for a day out, and claimed to have been racially abused by the bouncers of some nightclub.

Reclining in my seat I remember the same times that has happened to me in the past: those occasions when I was at a nightclub and harangued by a Pole or a Russian. Where jokes were made about the group of us, laughs had at our expense, and then we were turned away, often aggressively.

And I summon up a reminder that I live next door to several Eastern Europeans, and how standoffish they are. When I might say hello to them, they often just nod back, but I sense they are not sure what to make of me.

An image springs to mind as I study the article one last time: one of the New Britain that I live in, that new multi-cultural world, where the cultures all huddle together in uneasy company within the poorer areas of London, Leeds, Birmingham.

Maybe the article, maybe my world, is being played out before me on this trip, I hear my thoughts play.

"I wonder how I will cope here?" I say to myself.

The evening arrives with another group dinner, and another evening of mindless chatter. As I sit at the end of the table I spend most of my time watching the others talk about their day, or swapping more holiday stories, again with Robin and Tanya, yet this time I'm surprised by the fact they actually listen to me.

The main course arrives at just the time when someone decides to bring up my experience at the Cultural Centre.

"Enjoy your time going native?" Marco shouted from along the table. As I turned to him I noticed he held a sneering sort of smile.

"Marco!"

"What now Hazel? I'm only joking. He doesn't mind. You don't mind Karl, do you?"

I want to say yes, but find myself fighting an urge to tell this idiot to fuck off. "No, not at all." I turn to Hazel. "I enjoyed it really. Matthew showed me how to do something I'd never done before."

"Matthew?" exclaimed Marco. "You mean he even had an European name!"

"Lots of black people have European names, isn't that right Karl?" Hazel counters.

"Is Karl an European name?" one of the Americans asks.

"Well…"

"What was his African name?"

"Marco!"

"What now woman?"

"That is so un-PC."

"What? To ask what someone's original name is?"

"Yes!"

"Why?"

Hazel hesitated, looking around the table at everyone else, and suddenly going red with embarrassment. She even glanced at me, but I didn't have an answer for her either.

"It just is," she replied finally, as if that would close the subject.

"But there are plenty of black people who have disowned their slave names." It was Robin's turn to speak.

"What?" Marco said, taking another drink of wine.

"Look at the Nation of Islam for example. Plenty of their members denounced their 'Slave Names' and went back to choose something Muslim."

"Yeah, like Muhammad Ali. What was his original name?"

"Cassius Clay wasn't it?" said Tanya

"That's right. He denounced his name. Malcolm X was another, though I don't remember what his original name was."

As I looked around the table, feeling more and more uncomfortable, I noticed Kerry staring at me quizzically whilst holding her fork in her hand. As our eyes met, nothing was said, but I sensed something, something I noticed when she met me back at the bus earlier that day. Then her eyes went back to her food, and the link was broken, casting me back into this most useless, but most difficult, of conversations.

"And black people have come a long way in the world." Robin was still talking. "Look at Barack Obama. Hopefully, he will be our first black American President."

"No he won't," countered Tanya. "It will never happen."

The two girls turned to face each other. "Tanya. You always do this when we talk politics. You know he is the better person for the job."

"But he is black. We, I mean the whole of America; will never elect a black man to a job as important as that. Especially one with who might be a Muslim."

"What? Barack Obama is a Muslim?" someone else said.

"Yes."

"No Tanya, he is not. That is just a rumour put out by his rivals."

"He is!"

"How do you know that?"

"Because his middle name is Hussain. Everyone knows that."

I'd read about this argument many times before, but to see it played out before me was really quite astonishing. Two intelligent women, fighting a war of words within the War on Terror, and disagreeing over who should be the next President of the United States of America because one of the men in question had the wrong middle name.

As I smiled to myself, I glanced up at Kerry.

She was grinning as well. She rolled her eyes at to me, an act I took as her acknowledgement of the ludicrousness of the discussion running around the table.

"Well, I think the Americans will never elect a black President regardless of his middle name as well. I think they won't elect him because he isn't white and male." It was Marco's turn to add more fuel to the fire.

"What?"

"Well, just look what the French did when they had the chance to elect a woman who wanted to work for them," he continued, drinking more. "And look what they ended up with instead. A short man, who left his wife, remarried a beautiful woman, and then led them into a series of strikes that has paralysed Paris and most of the French rail system ever since."

"But there are other women in the world who hold positions of power," countered Robin. "Look at Germany. They have a female Chancellor."

Marco just snorted. "Yes, but even they struggled to elect her cleanly, giving her just enough power to form a coalition, and nothing more."

"So what are you saying?" I asked, finally finding my voice. "That a woman will always be elected over a black man?"

It was Robin who replied, whilst I hesitated. "Well yes. Clinton deserves to win the nomination, and it's about time a woman held a real position of power in the world. Did you see how sincere she was when she lost in Ohio, when she cried real tears? That is what a woman could bring to government, compassion and real feelings. She is a woman, and for too long women have suffered under men. She is a regular woman, just like me, and I can really relate to her."

I stared at her incredulously, thinking dangerous thoughts, reminding myself that Clinton wasn't any regular woman. She was the most privileged woman in America, and for that alone had nothing in common with most regular women, most black men, or most of the underprivileged people in the free world. I felt but didn't talk about how insulted I was by Robin's argument that because of her sex Clinton should win, that because of her sex I, a black man, should have voted for her were I American.

I also dared not to tell this young woman that using sexuality, race, or any other type of difference to win an election was a certain way of losing one. That from the minute you make your difference a call to arms you might win a few votes, but you then alienate whole swathes of others who don't, who can't, and who will never relate to you. A lesson painfully learned by Reverend Jackson and all the other black men who had run for office and failed.

I couldn't tell her, or the rest of the group, any of this, because I was scared.

"What I'm saying is that white men will always be in positions of power in the western world," Marco then said, around a mouthful of food. "That is how it has been, and that is how it will always be. I mean, just look at the benefits we have brought to the world: the industrial revolution, freedom and education to much of the world, economic wealth, the internet, world travel…"

"…two world wars, colonialism, slavery, nuclear weapons, famine, poverty, Global Warming, the list goes on."

We all turned to look at Kerry, who had by now put down her fork and was taking another sip from her wine glass.

"What do you mean?"

"What I mean is that men in the world, and in this case I mean white men, have brought as much pain as they have pleasure, as much hurt as they have comfort. So maybe we have all had enough and are looking for other ways of being in the world, all of us. Maybe we want to take the step to elect a female President in France, but are just a little nervous. Maybe America wants to try something different by electing a woman or a black man to sit in the White House as they are tired of what men have done before."

"Maybe the world is asking for something different," I added.

"Exactly," and then Kerry just looked around the table, taking another sip from her wine glass.

For a second we all seemed to be fixed in a kind of silence. The two Americans looked at each other, their mouths open, Hazel had her eyes cast downwards whilst Marco turned away, pretending to stare out of the window whilst chewing on a toothpick.

It was Randal who spoke up finally. "Please excuse my wife. She does this sometimes, creating arguments for no reason. Part of the reason I married her was because she is so opinionated, but occasionally she goes too far."

Like a bolt, I felt the patronising nature of his words, hoping I wasn't the only one. Watching the South Africans, I waited as Kerry just glowered at him, before she pushed back her chair, rose from the table, and left the room, slamming the door behind her. A few seconds later, Randal followed her, trailed closely by the American girls, both using the coming night out of clubbing as an excuse to remove themselves from the tension around the table.

"Well, that made for an interesting evening," Marco mumbled dryly, half-smiling at me.

I didn't return his gaze.

Four

When Ilse knocked at my door later that evening I had half a mind to stay in my room, especially after the prejudices played out around the table that evening. A part of me was furious, both with Marco and Tanya for their narrow minded vision of black people, let alone about women, and with myself, for not speaking my mind earlier or offering Kerry more support.

What she was suggesting was nothing new, yet it seemed to stimulate so much resistance when it came to light, especially amongst those not used to seeing or being around black people of worth or power.

But what really upset me most of all was how many of my friends and even my family held the same type of views. My own father would argue until the cows came home that no black man would ever make it into a position of power in the United Kingdom, the United States of America, or any other Western nation. Not without being assassinated or severely discredited along the way. It just wouldn't happen.

I was taught by my own parents that to be black meant that you had to be less than, that you had to know your place, or you would be reminded, often severely, just where that place was: normally several rungs of the ladder lower than the person doing the reminding.

It was as if the whip of that Overseer had been replaced by the tongue, or the undermining ways, of the western class system.

Shaking my head to remove myself from my resentment, I finally answered the door.

"Hi there," Ilse said, standing there in a black blouse, the top couple of buttons undone, and a pair of black trousers that showed of the curves of her figure. "Oh, are you not coming with me to the nightclub as we talked about earlier?"

"What?" I stammered, momentarily struggling for a reply. "I'm sorry. I was miles away, just thinking about what happened at dinner tonight."

"Yes, I heard about that. Robin told me when I saw her just now. Seems like there are some strong personalities in the group this year."

"You could say that again."

"Are you alright? Is there anything I can do to help at all?"

I smiled at her. "Thank you, but no. I don't think there is. They have their opinions and I have mine. I'm more concerned about Kerry than anything."

"I'm sure both herself and Randal will be fine," Ilse replied. Then she gave me the kind of smile I hadn't seen in her before, as if she was flirting with me. "If you like I can buy you a couple of drinks to help you recover from your ordeal."

"Oh really?" I said, finding her mood infectious, and given how I felt, pleasantly necessary.

"Sure. Tell you what. I will give you 15 minutes. Get ready and I will meet you in the lobby. I know a couple of good places to grab a beer here in Lusaka. Good local music too, so I'm sure you will like them. Deal?"

"Deal."

And half an hour later there we were, sat in a bar around the Northmeads Shopping Centre, a place crowded mainly with Zambian men and women in their twenties, by the looks of them. I felt like one of the older people there as I sat at the bar part talking to Ilse, part listening to the mixture of African and American music being played by the DJ.

"So, how long have you been running these trips?" I asked her over the noise.

"For about four years now," she replied. "I left Holland after university as I wanted to travel."

I took a sip from the bottle of beer, pleasantly surprised by its taste. "But why come to Africa? And why here?"

"Well, I don't just work in Zambia. After university I managed to get myself a job as a tour guide on trips out of Nairobi down to Mombasa and back. The company I work for liked me so much they put me on several of their other tours, through Tanzania, Namibia and Zambia. So here I am four years later, and I still enjoy it."

"All of it?"

"Well, most of it," Ilse smiled. "Sometimes I get a sense it might be time to go home, but I've based myself mainly in Lusaka now, so it's slowly becoming my second home."

"Mainly?"

"Yes, I have a house here, just on the outskirts of town, and also a good number of friends."

"Hence how you know this place."

Ilse nodded at me. "That's right. But what about you? What brings you to Zambia? We don't get that many black people coming from Britain. It's normally the middle and upper classes who come here, looking for a quick safari, and to be treated like royalty before going home."

I opened my mouth to reply honestly, but again found myself censoring my words. "I think I just needed a holiday. And Africa is a place I'd never been to before so wanted to try it before it gets too late."

"Well, I think you've made a good choice," Ilse said, holding up her bottle. "Cheers, and welcome to Africa."

"Cheers!"

I liked Ilse at that point, finding her pleasant, easy to talk to and good company. She reminded me of Sally back in London in that she was friendly, attractive and also slightly detached from me, things that drew me to a woman strangely enough.

And on occasion as we talked, the question did go through my mind if she was attracted to me or not. Of course I had a girlfriend at home (well, two), but I was on holiday, and what happened in Zambia would just stay in Zambia if I had my way.

After a couple of hours, Ilse suggested that she take me to another bar where we could actually dance, as the one we were in had now become so crowded that there was barely room to stand any more. We left, and walked for no more than five minutes, chatting casually on the way, until she turned right in to another doorway.

As we entered, she grabbed my hand, leading me through the throng of people all dancing to music with a purely Zambian flavour, and at her touch I found myself feeling more and more relaxed as we reached the bar.

"Take a seat," she shouted, pulling up a couple of bar stools.

"Thanks."

I watched as she called over to one of the barmen, a tall, broad shouldered guy, who seemed to do a double take when he saw us, first smiling, then looking a little quizzical. Slowly he walked along the bar whilst wiping a glass, before putting it down as he spoke to Ilse. I couldn't hear what they were saying, but their conversation seemed to go on for longer than the traditional length of taking our orders. I noticed that every couple of seconds he would glance over in my direction before saying several more words in Ilse's ear that she would reply to quickly.

"Anything wrong?" I asked once the bar man had walked away to grab us our drinks.

"Nothing really," Ilse replied, adjusting herself on her stool. "I just know that guy."

"Really? How come?"

"We dated for a short time recently. He didn't know I was back in Lusaka. Says that he would have called me if he had. He doesn't like you though."

"I gathered that," I replied, glancing up to see her friend the barman still glaring at me as he wandered back with our drinks, before he place them on the surface, took Ilse's money and ambled away to return to cleaning his glass. "Any idea why?"

"Cheers. Oh, I told him you were from England, and he is jealous of you being here with me."

"Why would he be jealous?"

"Because I want him to be," she laughed. "I told him we were together. You should have heard the words he had to say about you."

I suddenly felt shocked as I sat there, riveted to that stool, as I realised just what had taken place. This woman had used me, had used my colour to get back at her boyfriend, and I had fallen for it. Fallen for it like a fucking idiot, letting this young girl play with me, with myself and her boyfriend, and all for her own enjoyment. A part of me was furious at her, full of rage that she could have done this, that she could have her amusement with two men, two black men, asking us to almost joust for her favour, when neither of us knew the truth of the situation.

Ilse seemed to notice my sudden discomfort, placing a hand on my thigh. "I hope you don't mind."

"No," I lied. "No, I don't mind at all."

The next day was a rest day, so the morning afterwards we boarded our coach and took the six or seven hour drive south of Lusaka to

Livingstone. Sitting near the front of the coach I stared out of my window as we seemingly race along the road, past small dusty settlements, through sparse dry bush, and overtaking smaller buses packed full of commuters. I immersed myself in this scene of Zambia, so different to the vision of city life presented by Lusaka, with its rich skyscrapers and poor shack style housing all vying for possession of the land in many parts of the city.

The day before I'd spent most of the time recovering after my late night with Ilse, a night that culminated in my excusing myself and leaving the final bar we'd arrived at some fifteen minutes or so after her revelation that she was using me to get back at her boyfriend. I didn't tell her how I felt, though to be honest she never asked me. I was still so angry with me, angry that again I had not stood up for myself, angry that she could take a liberty like that with the pair of us.

In the late afternoon, whilst trying to avoid the rest of the group who I was fast coming to dislike, I took myself out for a walk through Lusaka. Walking for hours I drifted past the banks and the busy shops of Haile Selassie Avenue and Independent Avenue, before crossing the railway bridge and walking over to the railway station. Then along to the bus station where I sat and watched the dozens of porters and other chancers as they tried to carry bags, direct people to taxis, exchange money, and any other means of making a living one could think of.

Many times as I sat there watching, with a cold drink in my hand, I marvelled at the ingenuity of these people, at their energy and enthusiasm, and for the first time since I had arrived three days ago, I felt a sense of relaxation, of connecting to something real.

Now, as I sat there on that bus, I was back to my reality, and it was beginning to depress me. I hadn't seen the rest of my group the day before, and didn't really miss them if I was honest, so to have to hear Marco, Randal, and Kerry debating something else in the seats behind me just recalled to me how miserable I was becoming on this so called 'trip of a lifetime to Africa'.

"Look," Marco was saying. "It's here in the newspapers. Some parts of South Africa endure power outages for set times of the day as the country conserves its energy. That is what you get when you elect a black man as President."

"I know," it was Randal's turn to speak. "My country is in a real state right now, and I have no idea how we're going to sort things out. Mbeki seems to have made a real mess of things, and all he appears to be doing whilst crime rises and no one has electricity is interfering in the politics of our neighbours."

"Oh you mean that mess in Zimbabwe. You are probably right. Mbeki should stick to his own problems instead of attempting to play Africa's Number One Statesman. As for Mugabe, how is he still in power?"

"Well as long as the army is still on his side he can do whatever he wants, including starving his own people of food, and the rigging of elections. I hear there is to be a run off between him and his main opposition as even though he lost he didn't lose by enough votes."

"What do you think will happen?" Marco asked.

"Well, I suspect Mugabe will try to intimidate the voters to make them choose him, or attempt to rig the results again. He is a very sneaky and evil man that one."

"There you go then. Another reason these countries shouldn't be governed by themselves."

"You lot talk some shit sometimes," I then heard Kerry say.

"Kerry! Do you mind!?"

There was silence, before I heard Kerry add. "Ah, forget it."

And silence returned to our bus journey.

About two hours after we'd left Lusaka, whilst we were driving along a single lane road the bus seemed to suddenly develop a problem, with the engine spluttering and smoke rising from beneath us.

"What is wrong?" asked Ilse appearing concerned.

"I don't know," replied our driver. "I'm going to have to pull over and take a look."

"Alright."

The bus stopped on a dirt track at the side of the road and after pulling to a halt the driver hurriedly climbed out of the cab to have a look underneath.

"What's happening?" asked Hazel, appearing a little nervous at being out in the middle of nowhere.

Ilse stood to address us all. “I’m afraid we seemed to have developed a fault of some kind, but don’t worry, I’m sure our driver will have it fixed in a moment and we will be off on our way soon.”

I looked back at Hazel, who didn’t seem at all convinced by Ilse’s words, but remained seated in her chair, her arms folded, an irritated look on her face.

“So what do we do now?” shouted Marco belligerently.

“We should probably wait here on the bus,” Ilse answered. “Although if people want to alight they can do so, but I wouldn’t stray too far.”

“We could head down that road over there and see if they can help?” I heard Robin suggest.

“What?”

“There?” she repeated, pointing out the window at a sign in the fork of the road several feet away.

I could see a couple of my companions climb to their feet to gain a better view, peering out the window. I joined them, suddenly interested in visiting somewhere potentially more interesting than anywhere I had seen until now.

“That sign seems to be for an orphanage,” I said.

“Yeah. Let’s go and take a look. Come on Tanya.”

Then I watched as the Americans both rose from their seats and briskly moved towards the front door.

“Anyone else?”

“God no!” Marco replied.

“No other takers?” Robin asked for the final time.

I found myself sitting there transfixed, wanting to get up and join them, but not feeling as if I should, or as if it was allowed. It was left to Kerry to save me. “I’m coming too. You joining us Karl?”

“I’d love to,” I replied, trying not too appear too grateful.

As the four of us wandered down the dusty path towards a series of buildings in the distance, I could feel the anticipation of wanting to be around people who weren’t expecting to meet a tourist, and who wouldn’t then act in a special way accordingly.

I glanced around, noticing the sparse gnarled trees in this red brown setting, seeing them as pretty for the first time.

Smelling the heat and humidity as well as feeling it on my skin, sensing the comfort and ease return to me now I was off that damned claustrophobic bus. Just like those moments in the bust station I could feel my tension fade.

"Try not to let them get to you too much."

"What?"

"Marco and my husband," Kerry repeated. "Don't let them get you down too much. Randal can be pretty boorish at the best of times, but he doesn't mean it. He wouldn't have been able to become half the man he is today without South Africa being the way it is now. The changes we are all going through probably just scare him."

"And Marco?" I replied. "He doesn't seem to be just boorish, he seems downright hostile towards black people as a whole."

"Well I don't know about him. You would have to ask Hazel about that, but even she seems to be fed up with him at the moment."

"You noticed that too," I said smiling.

"Couldn't fail to. She had a face like thunder at dinner last night as he went on about something or other to do with the amount of crime committed by immigrants in London. She seemed really embarrassed by him, and even left the table early again, although this time she didn't say anything to him and just got up and stormed out. He looked absolutely stunned when she did it. Quietest I've seen him so far."

I allowed myself to laugh at that just a little bit. "Well, it's their marriage I guess. Each to their own."

Kerry chuckled with me.

We walked a bit further and rounded the first of a set of stone buildings with corrugated iron roofs, all lined up as if facing inwards, as if this was a type of compound. The area seemed deserted, but with obvious signs of the presence of people: numerous footsteps in the dirt, and clothes hanging up outside a couple of the buildings.

Tanya stopped in the road before us. "Can you hear that?"

The four of us all listened in, picking up the sound of singing and clapping coming from one of the buildings to our left, larger than the others, and set at the furthest edge of the compound.

Together we drifted towards the voices, recognising them as those of children, and as we approached the last structure we collectively peered through open window to see it was a crowded schoolroom. Seated cross-legged, these children of Zambia were singing and clapping and swaying in time. Singing a beautiful song that I didn't recognise, but with such grace and beauty that I could only feel joy.

At the other end of the room were the creators of the scene, two white nuns in their habits. The smiles on their faces spoke of love for the children before them, and the children's gazes reflected that love in equal measure. One of the women turned to us all. Without missing a beat she just nodded and smiled.

"You were right, it is an orphanage," Kerry whispered to me.

I nodded in reply, preferring to just continue listening to that sound radiating out of this large scruffy, shattered stone room in the middle of nowhere.

When the song was over the nuns talked to the children for a few minutes, during which time many of them noticed us the new arrivals at the window, pointing and giggling behind raised hands at the strangers in their midst. Then the nuns sent them outside to play. Dozens of boys and girls suddenly emerged from the room, all noisily running around or just standing around shouting, with some coming up to us to greet us, and others staying away as they appeared shy.

The two Americans seemed in their element as they chatted to a number of boys and girls who were intrigued by us, these new arrivals, whilst Kerry was holding a young boy in her arms who was no more than three years old. I watched her as she wiped away a sliver of snot that had begun to run down his face and which he had hungrily begun to lick at.

"Is this your first time in Zambia?" asked one of the nuns coming up to me.

I turned to look at her, noticing the kindly lined older face and her gentle manner. "Yes. My first time in Africa in fact."

"Then this must be quite an experience for you. Are you enjoying your time here?"

She must have seen the look on my face flicker, as her eyes seemed to bore into me for an instant.

"In parts," I answered. "May I ask your name?"

"I'm Sister Teresa. Myself and the sisters run this orphanage."

"I'm Karl," I replied politely. "How long has it been out here, in the middle of nowhere?"

"I think around fifty years now, and always staffed by the nuns. The church I work for sends us all over the world to do God's work."

"Must be hard with all these children."

"Sometimes it is, especially when they get ill, or when they come to us already quite sick. Then we do what we can to comfort them, but there is still a lot of pain when they finally depart for the promised land."

I nodded, seeing just a flicker of pain in her face for the first time. "Where do they come from?"

"Mainly Lusaka, but all over the country. They are often found wandering the streets by one of the charities that work with us, and because they know of others and us around Zambia they arrive here. Anyone up to the age of ten we will take. We can't take anyone older."

"But what happens when they are too old to stay here?"

"Then often they go to one of the cities to find work, but sometimes they end up on the streets again."

"Must be heartbreaking."

"It can appear that way. But often it is better to look at the positives. We do what we can for whom we can. That is all God asks of us, and all we can do."

I found myself smiling at her faith. "You're accent, are you Spanish?"

"Close. Italian. And you?"

"London, I'm British."

The conversation seemed to move away from the pair of us right then as Kerry wandered towards us, the young boy still in her arms smiling as she tickled him.

"Come and meet a friend of mine," she was saying to him, pointing in my direction.

The boy considered me cautiously, not entirely sure what to make of me, before burying his head into Kerry's shoulder.

"Oh, you are not that shy. Karl is a nice person."

I found myself smiling at this small black boy in a white South African woman's arms, feeling a connectedness to him.

"What is his name?" I asked Sister Teresa.

"This is John," she replied, before saying something to John in a language I didn't recognise.

John lifted his head, his big brown eyes again alighting on me. This time he seemed less unsure, but still wary, taking his time to study me, before glancing back at the Sister to check if I was safe for him to relate to.

"Good morning John," I said to him, tickling him on his belly.

John giggled shyly, pressing himself into Kerry even more.

"See," she said. "He does like you after all."

Then John turned to me and reached out with both of his hands, as if asking me to take him. I hesitated before grasping him, glancing at the Sister as if to check if I could.

"Go ahead," she prompted. "He wants you to hold him."

So, raising my arms, I met this young man, and pulled him gently towards me, holding him in my embrace at first as if I didn't know what I was doing, as if I was scared of breaking this delicate toy in my grasp. It was left to John to pull me closer, to wriggle in my arms until he was comfortable, to encourage my own disquiet to depart silently.

I suddenly felt as if this was something I had missed in my own life, that closeness and intimacy between a child and an adult, a parent. With a sudden sadness I realised I couldn't remember any of the times when, or if, my mother held me close to her chest, like I was doing now.

In an environment like this she would be one of the Sisters, always helping others, always finding a way to solve their problems, to make things right. It was rare I realised that she would cuddle me or come down on the floor to just play with me, like the American girls were doing across the courtyard. Her work as a prison counsellor meant that she would often take herself on jaunts around the jails of Britain. Trying to solve the problems of the black men encased therein whilst her son there outside played on his own each evening in his room, or whilst her husband beat her senseless in the days before and after I was born.

I found myself saying 'shhh' to the youngster in my arms as he shifted uncomfortably, as if he had sensed my growing tension.

As I looked down at him, he put a small hand against my cheek and touched my lips. Playfully I pretended to eat one of his fingers, making him laugh.

"See, he likes you," said Sister Teresa warmly.

Looking around, I noticed a nearby wall and wandered over to it. And with John still in my arms I sat there and we just talked and giggled as these beautiful, sad, British and Zambian children played, danced, and laughed with each other.

Interlude

Email
From: Lilly Tucker
Sent: 20th July 2008
To: Karl T

Had a few minutes at work and thought I would write you a couple of lines to say hello. Heard from Busta about what happened to your mother, and I'm really sorry to hear that, but I was surprised that you decided to go away so quickly.
Things here are as always, and work is still the same. The Director is on our case again about trying to move more people on from within the mental health system. He says it is becoming more and more difficult to get funding from the PCTs without some type of targets being put in place. They want greater accountability, so the world of mental health is changing. I'm not sure I like it, but what can I do? I need to survive, I have to look after Reggie, so I have to work.
Reggie is well though. His teachers gave him a good report last week, so I took him out to see a movie as a treat. It was an awful movie, but he enjoyed himself.

How is your mother by the way? No woman deserves what happened to her, so I hope she is well.

Lilly x

From: autonews@willesdenherald.co.uk
Sent: 23rd July 2008
To: Karl T

Knife crimes increase in borough!
Brent PCT recorded its highest rate of admissions for knife wounds since records began, it was announced this week. Their rate has risen by 20 percent since 2000, now placing them third in London. The new MP for Brent, Charles Jackson, said 'Londoners will be

shocked by the prevalence of knife crime in the borough which show the unacceptable side of the crime on Brent streets.'

Police hunt after partygoer is shot on train!

Several teenagers who were on their way home after a night of revelry were being sought after Bennie Davies, 17 years old, from Harlesden was shot in the leg in an alleged random and unprovoked attack. When returning from Wembley from a house party Mr Davies and several of his friends boarded a train at Wembley Central train and were accosted by other youths who were already present. A scuffle ensued and one of the youths already on the train pulled a gun out, firing it twice, and injuring Mr Davies. Mr Davies is now in hospital recovering from the wounds to his right leg and doctors are confident he will make a full physical recovery. Police are appealing for any witnesses to come forward.

Five

"Look at that lot over there!" Marco shouted, banging his large hairy hands together. "Those elephants, see? Look!"

"Where?" Hazel replied, whilst peering through a set of binoculars.

"Over there! Driver! Move in closer. My wife wants to see them!"

For the third time that day I glanced at Kerry, who was gritting her teeth to contain her irritation at this man seated in front of her. Marco seemed to have recovered from the argument in the jeep just moments before. He had also once again taken over the safari drive, but now his constant berating of our driver and guide was almost unbearable.

"Drive slower! Drive faster! Mind the potholes! Where are the animals? Get closer! Hurry up!" His endless demands were having their toll on the rest of us, and several times until now I'd played with the fantasy of throwing him out of the jeep or dangling him over the side for some lions to play with.

"Unfortunately," I discovered during a break as I talked to one of the guides about the type of game we might see, more out of personal curiosity than out of any real urge to get rid of Marco of course. "There are no lions in this National Park. But if we come nearer to one of the rivers there may be some Hippo or Crocodile lurking."

I smiled as I thanked him, the idea of several crocodile rolling around and ripping the idiot apart appealed to me even more, and comforted me as we walked back to our jeep to continue our drive through the afternoon.

When another bus had finally arrived to collect us from the side of the road, the journey down to Livingstone fell back into its uneventful groove.

Ilse apologised profusely for the three-hour delay in our journey, promising us all a free meal at the other end.

All I could do though was think about my experience back at the orphanage. Watching those children just be natural with each other was a joy I hadn't expected to experience on this journey of tourist sights and clichés, and sitting with John on my lap playing with that delightful little boy had left me feeling more than a little bit emotional. When Randal came down to tell us it was time to leave, I felt myself being torn in two. John even cried and gave me a final hug as I handed him back to Sister Teresa and her colleague who had joined us by that time. Finally though we said our farewells and departed: the American girls waving behind us enthusiastically at the children who had gathered to do the same: Kerry giving me a hug as I refused to turn around out of fear of losing myself emotionally.

It was nearly dark by the time we arrived at our walled compound in Livingstone: the bus driver once again honking his horn at the large and locked whitewashed gates, before a uniformed security guard forced them apart to allow us entrance.

Expressing regret once again at the delay, Ilse led us all inside and hurried up the formalities of our checking in, before we all departed to our room, exhausted, but just happy to have finally arrived.

The next morning everyone seemed to have recovered their enthusiasm for the trip a bit, with Robin and Tanya particularly unaffected by the previous day, as they chatted happily with Hazel and the Kerry about their experiences at the orphanage. Marco though was just as irritatingly belligerent as always, as he bullied a young serving girl into providing him with his morning scrambled eggs just the way he wanted them, sending her away with them three times.

I thought about him as the conversations continued around that breakfast table, finding it hard to imagine that thick irritating man ever being anything other than brash and standoffish with a group of children like the ones we had met. With his oafish ways, and his constant belittling he didn't seem to have the capacity to care for anything or anyone at all it seemed. I even wondered just how Hazel had put up with him for all this time, even though they had been with the R.A.F. and had a couple of children of their own.

It left a warmish feeling that sense that I might be better than him, that I might be more than this crude man. I couldn't help but revel in the feelings.

We were to be in Livingstone for three days, spending today on safari, and tomorrow at the Victoria Falls, with the following day being a free day to do so as we wished, before travelling back to Lusaka for a couple of days of further excursions and then returning home.

I felt fine that morning, if a little melancholy. My feelings hadn't returned to normal, and I felt noticeably different.

It barely registered when the time came for us to finally depart. We were split into two groups, with the Americans, Ilse and Randal going in one and myself, Marco and Hazel, and Kerry riding in the other.

The two jeeps took about twenty minutes to reach the main gate of the Mosi O Tunya National Park, with Ilse's group leading the way in order that she could pay the entry fee for both our vehicles.

As we drove through the park I could feel the energy rise in our jeep, as if we were all excited at the prospect of finally seeing some game. It wasn't long therefore until we came across several zebra that were quietly eating away and ignoring the obvious sounds of humans and their vehicles approaching.

"Wonderful," I whispered to myself, feeling a growing awe at a scene I couldn't have come across in Europe.

"Can't we get any closer?" Marco was fighting with a large camera, trying to clumsily take a picture before the animals moved away.

The driver manoeuvred us slightly forward so he could get a better view.

"Is that all?"

"We're not allowed to go to close to them," the driver replied, a polite man who didn't tell us his name but said he lived in Livingstone and gave us bits of information about the area. "It is so that we do not scare them."

Marco stared at him incredulously. "I don't care what the rules are, I want you to get closer to them. I pay you to do as I say, not what the rules might say you should."

"Marco…," questioned his wife, clearly starting to feel embarrassed.

"What?"

The driver raised a hand in compliance before driving as slowly as he could to get closer to the animals before us, who seemed thankfully unaware of our intentions. Then Marco finally managed to focus his camera and take several pictures, before sitting back in his chair beaming triumphantly.

"There you go. Told you I would get some good shots for my collection."

Hazel just about managed a thin smile.

The driver then took us away through the park, following what seemed like well-worn tracks through the trees, and simultaneously speaking on his radio to his colleague in the other jeep.

After a short while there seemed to be a series of more urgent words shared between the two groups, and our driver took a sharp turn in the path, driving marginally faster than he had been before, as if he was in a hurry to get somewhere.

"What's going on?" I asked.

"My colleague has spotted one of the rhino."

"Really?" I smiled. "Great."

"Well come on then," Marco interrupted. "You had better hurry up. Don't want to miss them."

After barely a few minutes we were approaching what seemed to be a set of albino rhino, four of them all standing by, the two adults watching over their two young as they ate and played.

"They're beautiful," whispered Kerry beside me.

I nodded, feeling that sense of awe rise within me again.

Even Hazel whispered to herself as she saw them.

"Come on!" Marco shouted, totally shattering the silence. "Just like last time. Get us in closer!"

"Sir," replied the driver. "These are rhino. They do not like it if we come too close. Especially when they are caring for their young."

"I don't care if they're guarding the Crown Jewels themselves. Just do as I say, man!"

I could see Kerry rolling her eyes. Hazel glanced at us, her embarrassment growing.

With a sigh, and again not wanting to cause an argument, our driver slowly moved a bit closer to the four animals.

I could see that one of the rhino was looking at us, its horn sharp and angry, its eyes fixed on our small, suddenly brittle jeep.

"Is that all?" said Marco incredulously.

"Sir..."

A blast of noise across his radio stopped the driver from doing anything else. Answering it, he spoke quickly for a moment, before putting his vehicle in reverse and pulling away.

"What are you doing?"

"Sir, the other jeep warned us that the bull rhino there is about to charge unless we back away."

"No he won't. Go back up there."

"Sir..."

"Do as I say!"

"Oh shut up!"

Even I felt shocked as I heard my own voice echo off the metal walls of that jeep and everyone turned to look at me, including the driver.

But I was lost by this point, my calm shattered by this idiot of a man, so I continued. "All I've heard you do since you got here is bully and criticise anyone who has tried to help you. From the waiters to the driver here, you just keep on goading and pushing, knowing full well that none of them would ever push back. No they are far too polite for that. But do you respect that, do you show them any respect in return. No, all you ever do is carry on as if you're some kind of overseer and now that you're here in Africa, these are your slaves."

"Do you mind," started Hazel, surprisingly leaping to the defence of her husband.

"Oh don't worry about me," Marco interrupted, turning to glare at me. As our eyes met, he just sneered at me. "I can look after myself. This fool thinks that because he has come here to Africa for the first time, because he is here on this tour with us, he has the right to criticise me for being a colonialist. As if his brief sojourn to that orphanage yesterday gave him a better idea of who he is and why he is here. As if him holding the hands of a few snotty nosed black brats makes him better than me.

"You don't think I know your sort do you Karl. You don't think I've ever met anyone who felt as lost as you, who wanted to come to Zambia to rediscover a part of themselves. But I do know you. And I know that you are no better than me because you are here in this sanitised little bubble, staring out at Africa, not really getting involved in it. You are here because you are too afraid to be out there amongst the poverty and the wildness of Africa. You are too afraid because you are just too British to be anything else."

I stared at him, seething as I was, as he watched me with a smug triumphant smile on his face.

"Feel free to tell me that I'm wrong at any time," he finished calmly.

"You are so wrong. You have no idea about me." It was the best I could manage, and even then I knew it was a lie.

I was here in Africa on this trip because I wanted to be, because I wanted to discover a part of myself that they tell us we've lost hundreds of years ago. Yet all I'd managed to do was to float through it like a balloon through a storm, to drift along on the breeze, not really letting myself be buffeted by the winds, struck by the lightening, or ripped apart by any hurricane coming. Besides my time at the orphanage when I actually felt something: when for the first time since I'd started this journey I allowed myself to connect with something real and tangible, all I had done was stay safe, stay apart from, stay Western.

As I stared at Marco, I realised that he had seen through me and beaten me, and I hated him for it.

When the safari ended a couple of hours later, I felt exhausted. Not just from being out in the warmth of the jeep all day, but also from having to sit and listen as Marco bullied his way through the rest of the ride, often aggressively cajoling the driver to do his bidding whilst the rest of us were now just forced to watch and listen.

It was a relief therefore when we arrived back at the compound. As I stood in the shower later, allowing myself the chance to just revel in the water, to just wash off that days dirt, I couldn't help but play back the words Marco had said so forcefully to me.

That evening, after checking my emails, I decided not to eat with the others, choosing instead to take a book with me and go and sit in a bar or restaurant nearby somewhere. I walked for twenty minutes, slowly taking in the sights of a calm evening in Livingstone, before spotting the sign for a large restaurant Ilse had recommended to me a couple of days previously.

On entering, a polite young lady showed me to a table not too far from the bar. I ordered a meal and a beer and sat back, looking around the room. Several of the tables were empty, but at least half the room was full of people. Couples, and groups of men and women, some tourists some not, spread themselves out within the large space.

I felt particularly envious of a group of Zambian men who were seated at the bar, watching a television screen that seemed to be showing something from the British Premier Football League. There was lots of gesticulating, waving of arms, groaning at the missed scoring opportunities, and cries of dismay at any dubious refereeing decisions. I smiled as I watched them, realising they were no different to the men at home in Harlesden.

Surprising myself, I then found my thoughts drifting to my father, and his view of black men. How he viewed them as unruly, with no discipline, and lacking in respect for their elders and even themselves.

"I don't know what is wrong with them," I remembered him saying to me over one of the few dinners we shared, some several years ago now. "There they are, out on the streets at all times, their jeans hung low, pants showing. Now what sort of style is that? And what in the heavens makes them think they can get away with all the stabbings and shootings that seem to be going on all over the place? They have no respect for anyone. I think they must be sick the lot of them."

I remember how animated he was as we talked back then. How angry he was at these black men for bringing disrespect onto the rest of them, the rest of us. I recollected how angry he was at the government for not doing more to help us, to assist the community in changing, in fighting, what was going on within. And I can still hear the arguments he would have with my mother about whether or not religion was a means to a better life for us all, as if believing in God and asking his assistance would mean he would save us.

And yet I couldn't help but wonder about all the reasons he seemed to give for their infractions. There seemed to be one missing to me, perhaps the largest, most important one of all, and my father felt like he was steering himself away from it.

At no time did he blame himself. At no time did my father, that representative from his generation, present himself and his peers as the reason for the failures of my own. At no time did he own up for their disappointing relationship with their own children. At no time did this wife beater, child abuser and general philanderer ever admit to having played such a large part in letting his children down.

I recall how afraid I was of him as a child. How the very atmosphere used to change when he entered a room at the end of his day at work. How he would march in, his face stern, his body stiff and erect, his demeanour discouraging of any type of intimate interaction from his children. I remembered how he would sit in his chair, turn the television over to the news, and just sit there, ignoring me, distant from me. And how many of the times when he did talk to me involved some type of criticism or put down.

There was no bouncing on his knee, no telling of romanticised tales from his childhood. There was never any rough and tumble in the park, or being taken out into the garden and taught how to help him maintain it.

He was a challenging man to get to know, a distant man, a man I walked on eggshells around, and even though many of my friends told me I should have been glad to have had a father around for so long, many times did I wish him dead.

I was angry with him still for what he did to my mother, I understood that, but perhaps I was always angry with him directly too. Maybe I always had these feelings towards him, the sense that we didn't like each other, that we were never going to be close. But there was no space in our relationship for honest expression. These were the type of feelings that one had to hold close to one's chest at all times. You couldn't be angry with your father, you couldn't tell him that you hated him. No. That would have resulted in a beating with the belt, and with being told how useless or shitty I was. That would have led to my mother to take my father's side and chastise me herself as well.

So any feelings I might have had about him, be they positive or otherwise, were always suppressed. I had to hide what I felt about my father, gulp it down when it threatened to come to the surface. I had to contain myself through the years of depression when I was in a teenager, and through the times when I got into trouble with the police myself in my late teens.

My meal arrived as my thoughts moved on to what it must be like for us all. What must it be like in a culture where either we are afraid of our fathers or we just don't know them. What must it be like for the boys and women I grew up with to have no knowledge of a man who cares, who loves them, who shows them what it is to be a man. What must it be like for a woman who has no idea about what a man is supposed to be like as she didn't have a decent one in her life. What must it be like for that man, for that women, and how would they ever be expected to grow into something real. Something more than just a generation of bling, something more than just an age group of the booty called and teenage pregnant.

At what stage would my father and his contemporaries finally take responsibility for letting down a generation of boys and girls: those now often destructive men and occasionally misguided women, with their selfishness and their anger at the world.

I aggressively sawed, cut and chewed at my food as I recalled him. I remembered the arguments we used to have, often about things that weren't important. Often around the times when a son should listen to his father: when he should on occasion be heard by him.

Like the time when I was fourteen and choosing my subjects for my Ordinary Level Examinations: a key moment in a boy's life that was supposed to shape me. And there we sat, at the dining table, me with this man who had spent no time previously helping me with my homework, or coming to see me play football.

Me and this adult of a man, this man I was already scared of. Him telling me what subjects I needed to take to become an accountant, me telling him I wanted to do the subjects I was good at to become an artist. Our two opposing stances leading that discussion to degenerate into him yet again berating me: me yet again trying to explain myself: and him yet again coldly criticizing me further. Until my tears came, until I relented, until I went to my room and raged in those four walls, cried my eyes out, and slept. Until I did as he told me to: failed my exams, left school, started college, hated it and never went back.

This bastard of a man, this man who I always feared: please meet the man who sabotaged me. Let me show you the men who damaged us.

Where does that anger go?

Where do those feelings of fear for one's father dissipate to?

Or do they just stay hidden within us?

Are they what drive these kids back home to perform the way they do? Is their fear and their anger part of the reason they gather together in gangs, or part of the reason they feel the need to have a Rotweiller living with them in a council flat? The boys who stab boys, who shoot boys, who fuck over boys. Is this fear of their male elders a reason they need each other, yet fear each other?

And for these girls, who fuck boys, who become pregnant with child, who leave boys. Is their fear of their male elders a symptom of their desire to have, yet haste to leave the boys in their lives? Is their lack of containment a warning sign to authority, to the world?

Finally, I finished my meal and sat back before ordering another beer. Giving myself a break from my musing I found myself drawn again to the television and watched the fast paced football match being played back home. And as I sat there, as the game progressed, I watched the small group of men seated before the screen, riveted by the scene being played out before them.

But it is when they panned in on the crowds in the football stadium back home that I found myself finally understanding something. As I heard the chants, sensed the belligerence, and felt the goose bumps on my skin rise, I got that part of it. As I saw the men and women together, groups, gangs, and aggression, all contained within that modern day amphitheatre.

"That is how it should be," I whispered to myself surprisingly.

I didn't understand why I said that, all I knew was that I was right.

Six

The next morning I skipped breakfast and stayed in my room, staring out of the back window at the plant life outside. I didn't want to sit with Marco and the others, I'd decided, and had almost fully withdrawn from the rest of the group following yesterday's almost altercation.

It was only when Ilse came to my room that I realised it was time for us to leave.

"I noticed you didn't join us this morning?" she said, trying to sound casual as we walked towards the bus.

"That's right."

"I heard a rumour about something happening in your jeep yesterday. Is everything alright?"

"Of course it is," I lied.

She stopped to look at me, and our eyes momentarily locked. Hers with me, one of her guests on the trip: mine with this woman who used me in the nightclub last week.

"Listen Karl, I just need to say that if there is anything you need to talk about whilst you are here then you know you can do so. If there are any problems then don't hesitate to tell me."

I smiled for her, in an attempt to put her at ease. "I won't."

Climbing onto the bus I nodded a quick hello to Kerry and the American girls. Kerry smiled back up at me warmly, whilst Tanya and Robin make their best efforts to do the same, their eyes red and bleary from what seemed to have been yet another late night out on this trip. Then I took my seat, and the driver started the engine, pulling us out into the busy morning traffic of Livingstone.

The journey to Victoria Falls was thankfully short, and as we approached several of the group spotted elephants and other animals in the brush along the side of the road. Then, with a wall of white seemingly rising out of the ground some way ahead, Ilse rose and stood triumphantly at the front, as if she were about to deliver a little speech.

"We will spend maybe half of the day here at the Falls, so feel free to take your time and look around."

The driver then turned off the road, and entered an area lined with numerous stalls seemingly selling exactly the same things. I caught myself mentally calling them tourist traps, seeing them as if manned by men from all parts of Africa, here to make some money of their own from us wealthy Western travellers.

"Scavengers," I heard Marco say, glancing at Randal, then towards me.

As we pulled to a stop, and the door opened, accessing us to the noise of the waterfall beyond, they congregated on us, dozens of them.

"I wish they would just leave us alone," mumbled Hazel irritably.

In the end we followed Ilse, forcing our way through the numerous hawkers and beyond to the entrance gate, where we all signed in as our guide paid our fees for us.

It was then that I left the others, choosing again to do my own thing as I walked down towards the roar that had been growing in my ears since I arrived here at this natural wonder. I followed the track laid out before me, pursuing those people up in front of me who I didn't know, whilst all of us gazed out longingly at this sight, all of us barely talking, as if in quiet awe.

But as I stared out at the wall of white falling hundreds of feel onto the beaten rocks below, I spotted the trees at the top, noticing the specks of people dancing amongst them, seemingly at the falls edge.

Drawn towards them, I stopped on that path, then retraced my steps, skipping as if in a hurry to get up there. It was as if I needed to see them, to have the view they did, and to be up there, on the lip of the falls itself.

For a strange few minutes I didn't feel like myself, I felt different, liberated.

Then when I saw them my doubts returned. The three girls and their friends, all happily playing in the waters of these falls, all happily, fearlessly, dancing from rock to rock. With no health and safety they chatted, laughed, frolicked, and just enjoyed themselves.

Seeing me, and my blackness, they called out to me, and asked me to join them: these kids of maybe half my age talking in the most friendly of ways to a tourist, a black man up here on his own.

In the end, I took off my sandals and sat there with my feet in the water. Gripped by my British reserve, I dangled my feet in the warm waters of the Victoria Falls as if it was an August day and I was an elderly tourist on the beach in Margate.

"You fucking idiot," I whispered to myself with half a smile, as if catching my own criticism.

Pushing myself, and because I liked the feel of it, I took off my t-shirt, put my wallet into my bag, and with my shorts still on, I waded out into the water. Enjoying the warmth I found myself quickly relaxing, grinning to myself in an almost inane way as I paddled out to meet those others.

I looked up to see them standing on some nearby rocks pointing at me, beckoning me towards them, laughing as I laughed, clapping as I warily treaded water.

Then, as I clambered onto one of the rocks nearest them, they applauded me, cheering me for my efforts. I felt exhilarated. Pleased with myself for completing something I had so wanted to do for the first time since I'd arrived here in this strange land.

"Well done," one of the girls said in her strange accent, nodding her head back towards the shore. "They never come to join us out here."

"Really?" I replied, glancing back behind me. There on the bank were some of my group, including Marco and Kerry. Both were smiling, though I guessed for very different reasons.

"Are they your friends?" the girl continued.

"No, they are just on the same tour as me."

"I don't like them. They don't seem very friendly to me."

I studied them as well. "No, they are not really. All except a couple of them."

"They why see Africa with them?" the girl asked, as if knowing something of me.

I hesitated. "I don't know," I replied finally.

I spent maybe an hour out there on the rocks, amusing myself by trying to swim as far as I could out towards the lip of the falls, whilst the girl and her friends went off and played. In the end, and fearing that I might take one step too far, I returned to the shore, allowing myself to just sit there in the sun and dry off as I read one of the books in my bag. Then finally, it was time to return to my coach, so waving goodbye to the group that had so warmly welcomed me, I put on my t-shirt and sandals and walked back along the bank towards the exit to the falls.

"Didn't think you were going to come back now you'd gone native," Marco quipped as I entered the bus.

"Fuck off," I said calmly, not really in the mood for any of his nonsense after my first meaningful experience on this trip.

The rest of the group seemed shocked by my reaction, all except Kerry and the Americans I noticed.

"He was only joking," Hazel interrupted, protecting her husband again.

"Sure he was," I replied dryly. "Like he always is. Always with some put down for me, always with something nasty to say about someone here."

Hazel looked at me nervously, her handbag gripped tightly on her lap, then she shifted her gaze and stared out of the window. Marco meanwhile just glared at me with sheer hatred in his eyes.

I chose to ignore the pair of them and went to find a seat at the back, and on my own.

The following day I went out early and just wandered through the town of Livingstone, seeing what I wanted to see, and sitting in bars just watching the world go by. Then on our third day near the falls we returned to Lusaka on another bus ride, although this time without any delays or breakdowns.

Our time back in Lusaka included another day of optional excursions that I didn't take part in, prior to us then having a final dinner together. It was to have been the whole of the group sitting around a table to celebrate our visit in Zambia, and to reminisce about our time as a unit.

Again I didn't join in, feeling the depth of loathing towards most of the group, and knowing that I wouldn't at any other time want to be around them, so why now. And when Ilse handed me a Feedback Form for her organisation, I thanked her politely, but secretly said to myself that I wasn't going to complete it.

During that final day, I decided to go out for a walk over the railway bridged, turning left so I could again see the financial centre of the town. Ambling past some familiar banks, I for the first time noticed the armed security guards standing outside of them. Puzzled, I looked around for someone to ask as to why, but didn't see anyone I felt would understand just what I wanted to know, so I just walked on down the road.

Feeling suddenly hungry, I stopped at a fast food place, somewhere selling chicken, but as I walked inside I heard my name being called.

"Karl!"

Turning round I noticed Kerry standing alone half way across the other side or the wide road and waving at me. As I returned her gesture, she seemed to take that as meaning she should continue coming in my direction and join me.

"How are you?" she asked pleasantly enough.

"I'm good," I replied calmly. "Just about to grab myself something to eat."

"Excellent. I'm starving too, and dinner isn't until late tonight. Mind if I join you?"

Reluctantly, I agreed to her request, and we went inside together, ordering at the counter, before the lady serving us gave us our drinks and a ticket and bade us to sit down.

"I'm glad I ran into you," Kerry said once she'd taken a sip out of her bottle of Coke. "You haven't really seemed too happy in the group these past couple of days. I wanted to ask you how you were but wasn't sure if I should."

"Well if I'm honest, I'm not enjoying being around most of those idiots. I don't mind yourself and the two girls, but the others just really get on my nerves."

"Including Randal?"

"Oh I'm sorry," I stammered, not wanting to upset her.

"Don't be. He can be a real pain in the ass, and at times he has some very narrow-minded views about black people."

"And yourself?"

I watch as she shrugged, taking a second to think before she answered. "Well, I'm a bit more open minded, mainly because I've worked amongst them for more than twenty years now. My work as a doctor was in one of the townships, not in some surgery within the city."

"Must have been tough."

"No more than anywhere else in medicine," Kerry countered. "But I enjoyed the feedback I got from my patients.

They were more giving, more thankful and loving, than the majority of those I met when I worked in the city. I valued that, and sometimes I miss it."

"What made you leave?"

"Randal's work. He was asked to move to another area of the country, and was offered more money to do so. Of course I had to go with him."

"Are you happy?"

"Most of the time," she said smiling at me.

We continued chatting as the food arrived, generally just making small talk about our respective lives in South Africa and Britain, before she asked the question I dreaded she would fire at me.

"Karl, there is one thing I don't understand," she started quizzically. "What is it that brings you out here? You seem to be looking for something."

"How do you know that?"

"Don't try to hide it. It's in your eyes."

Right then it was as if she had seen through me. It was like she was reading me and I had revealed all of myself to her without even knowing it, and it scared me.

"I'm sorry," she continued, maybe noticing my embarrassment.

"Don't be," I countered, rescuing her slightly, perhaps because I was beginning to trust her. "I'm here because of problems at home, and because I feel I need to be."

I watched as she grabbed a napkin and dabbed her mouth. "I thought as much. You have a certain look about you, as if you have lost something.

"I guess I do," I replied.

"Then do you feel you've found it on this trip?"

I almost laughed as she asked me the most serious question of our conversation.

"I didn't think so."

"How did you know?"

"Because you seemed more and more frustrated the longer we've been out here. The only time I've truly seen you be yourself was at the orphanage the other day. With that child in your arms you were so much more relaxed, and less self conscious, than you are now, even with me."

I sat back in my chair and just stared at her, perhaps countering her statement by acting a little too cocky, "Alright then. What do I do?"

"I'm not going to tell you that," Kerry laughed, shaking her head. "You need to come up with a decision that works for you. If you really want to find yourself out here in Africa then do so, but do it properly. Not on a trip like this one. Not in some type of cultural bubble where everything is sanitised to make it seem nice and fluffy."

"But I thought you liked the safari and the trip to the falls."

"And yes I do, but there is no grit to it," she continued, rubbing her thumb and forefinger as if to emphasise the point. "It is all very safe on this journey. That is why I came out here on my own. To get some kind of feel for the real Zambia, not the tourist version, minus Aids, minus the Chinese influence, and without the poverty and struggles of normal people. That is Randal's way of living not mine and sometimes I find it quite stifling. I wanted, no needed, to experience something deeper, at least for a couple of hours."

I looked at her right then. Her mouth was contorted and the shine in her eyes gave her a deeper look than at any time since I'd met her. It astonished me, but I also liked it, sensing that we maybe had something in common at that point.

"I think I did too," I said finally.

"No Karl," she countered. "I think you need something more."

We finished our meal and then went back out into the late afternoon heat, the conversation returning to our respective lives in our own nations. We walked for ages, swapping stories, and comparing notes about the ways our lives were both similar and different. Then, occasionally, Kerry would stop and point out something in a shop or being sold by someone on the street, and explain to me just what was happening out here in Lusaka. I was being given a hint of Zambia from someone who knew Africa, but only a hint.

"Tell me something," I asked her as we passed another bank, and another set of armed guards. "What is that all about? Is it really that unsafe around here?"

Kerry laughed. "Totally safe, though you wouldn't think it to see the number of guns they carry.

"Oh really?" I knew that I didn't look particularly convinced.

"Well there is rarely any trouble, and besides, it is cheaper here to have men at the front door with a gun in their hands than it is to have all the nonsense that you have at home."

I stopped in the road, suddenly shocked. "You're joking."

"Not at all. Remember, the cost of living out here is less than in Europe, so the wages are less. Then, to buy and put in place all of the cameras and othyer technological stuff you have back home costs millions of pounds. A country like this doesn't have those types of resources. It's often cheaper, and maybe even safer, to have a system like this one."

"And I don't even feel that safe at home most of the time," I added.

"Exactly. It's like not having policemen walking the streets and replacing them with electronic equipment, like cameras at every corner monitoring everything and everyone. Sometimes you need to have a physical presence in place to feel positive about life.

"Let me tell you a story. I have a cousin in Manchester who told me about that Tory Political Party MP who decided to resign his seat in reaction to all of the security you guys have back there. Isn't that right?"

"Yes. I think I've heard the story."

"Well apparently, he quit because you now have a rule whereby you can hold anyone in detention for up to forty-two days, anyone at all. You also have National Identity Cards coming around the corner, and apparently you have one CCTV camera in place for every fourteen people living in the country. That's around five million of them all balancing on poles within one small island. Now can you imagine how much all of that stuff actually costs? Millions of pounds I'm sure. And as you've just said, you don't actually feel any safer."

"I see your point."

It was Kerry's turn to stop and look at me. "Do you really? I don't think so Karl. Let me be honest with you. I think you are as scared here as you are there, only you don't know it. I think you have always been scared, hence why it's taken you so long to open yourself up to people out here, both in our group and outside of it. Because, just like the rest of our group in their holiday bubble, you are absolutely terrified of anything different to that you already know."

I could feel myself growing with anger at her, whilst another part wanted to thank her, the pain of the pair seemingly boxing for the world title of my soul in that minute. Yet I also knew she was right. That this holiday for me was nothing more than an excuse to try and do something I wanted to say I'd done, not to actually engage with it for real.

This was an opportunity to see a country I'd been frightened into dismissing as a child, but even now as an adult I was still alarmed by it. My distance from it kept me that way, and even though I'd learnt more about Lusaka in the past couple of hours with Kerry than I'd experienced at any time previous to this, I had barely even bumped its surface. And now, with my last night in Africa approaching, I was about to leave somewhere I didn't know any greater than I had before, and I felt ashamed of myself.

Seven

"What is this?"

Marco was once again berating one of the serving girls about something, and try as I might to ignore him, it seemed impossible to shut out that irritating voice from entering my head.

"That is what you ordered sir," the serving girl replied. "A steak done medium rare."

"It looks like it's been overcooked," Marco replied, before leaning down to smell his meal. His sniffing sound came across like a vacuum cleaner does when it gets blocked. "And it doesn't smell too fresh either. Get me another one."

"Certainly sir," said the girl politely, before removing herself quickly from the dining room.

It was later on that evening.

Following my conversation with Kerry, I'd reluctantly decided to come along to my group's meal on our last night in Zambia. In between our return and my arrival at the table I'd been doing a lot of thinking about the things Kerry had said to me.

She had touched on something, I realised, not just about me, but about others like me, with all our idealised impressions of this land, and its peoples. But very few of us seemed to truly take the time to delve any deeper, and maybe that was because we were actually afraid of what we might find here.

In a perfect world, all I wanted to do therefore was to spend some time and just work out what was next for me, and also to avoid any type of confrontation with Marco or anyone else.

I was reminded as soon as I heard the idiot at the end of the table that it was a vain hope from the moment my mind suggested it, and with a sigh, I went back to listening to the conversation at my own end.

"We've had such a great holiday," Tanya, the American, was saying in agreement with her friend Robin. "I loved the day out at Victoria Falls. That was such a magical sight."

"And I loved the safari we all went on," Robin added. "Seeing all of that wildlife just reminded me of what we miss out on at home."

"And what about the idea of volunteering out here?" Kerry asked them.

"Well Tanya isn't so sure about that anymore, are you?"

"No, not after seeing all of the poverty," her friend agreed.

"But I still want to take a year out from my time at college and work here. I so loved being around the children at the Orphanage. I would so love to do something like that."

She turned to me, and I found myself smiling at her youthful enthusiasm to venture out into a world she didn't know or understand any more than I did, a world she was willing to embrace more than her friend.

"Well good for you," I said to her finally. "I hope you get the chance to."

"Thank you."

"And you Karl," added Tanya. "What will you do next when you get home?"

I thought about her question, pondering it. I'd been bothered by that subject myself ever since I'd come back to the hostel with Kerry just a few hours earlier, with only one answer presenting itself.

'But you can't,' a part of me whispered to myself. 'You have to go home as you have a job to do.' And when I would try to fight, it would say, 'You have a mortgage,' or 'Lilly and Reggie need you.' And if all those arguments failed then the ultimate line would be, 'and what about your mother?'

"I'm not sure as yet. I need to think about things, but I have a couple of ideas about what I want to do next."

"Do you want to tell us what they are?" the girls asked.

"Not yet," I replied smiling.

As I glanced across the table, I could see Kerry looking at me intently as I answered the girl's questions. I had the funny feeling she was again seeing into me. It was as if what she saw something almost met with her approval.

Just then, we all turned our heads as the waiter appeared. We watched as he hurried over to the table and spoke quickly to Ilse, who rose and followed him back into the kitchen.

"Must be trouble brewing," Kerry remarked.

"I hope not. It's been such a nice trip so far, I just hope they are not going to spoil it," Tanya added.

I didn't ask her who 'they' actually were.

Eventually, Ilse returned from the kitchen, and walked over to where Marco and Hazel were sitting, kneeling between them before speaking to them as quietly as possible so as not to disturb the rest of the group.

Suddenly Marco banged his fist down on the table. "What? That fucking wanker has no right to treat me like this!"

As the others turned to see what was going on, I noticed Hazel looking a little nervous. Ilse though, just continued talking to him as calmly as possible, meaning we still couldn't hear her.

"Well, you need to go back in there and tell him that I want my food the way I want it! Not the way he wants me to have it!"

"Sir, he says you've complained about every meal you have asked for since you've been here," Ilse replied, her voice slightly more audible now.

"And that little fool works for me. I've paid a lot of money for this trip…"

"As have others sir. All I'm asking is for you to go a bit easier on the staff here. They've worked very hard to keep you happy."

"Like fuck they have!" the idiot shouted. "Those fuckers are nothing more than animals, the lot of them!"

"Sir…"

"Ever since I've arrived in this godforsaken place I've been reminded of just why I hate them so much. You ask for something and they take an age to do it. They're lazy, inefficient, and rude. No wonder things have gone downhill since the Europeans left!"

I noticed Tanya glance at me nervously.

"Sir…"

"No. You let me continue. You've done nothing for us on this trip. Every time my wife has asked you for something you've told her you couldn't do it. Well you go back into that kitchen young lady and tell that waste of space to come out here and talk to me himself, and I will give him a piece of my mind and put him in his place!"

"Sir…"

"Just do it!" Marco roared, his large face now fully red, his eyes looking as if they could literally pop out of their sockets.

We all jumped as he said it, even Ilse, but none of us said anything to help her. We just stared at the pair of them as they regarded each other. Then Ilse glanced around the table, noticing all of our attentions, before she stood and returned into the kitchen.

For a short while silence reigned around the table, before his wife decided to say something. "Dear…"

"Don't!" Marco replied sharply. "I don't want to hear it. Not now, not later! I hate the fact you made me come here, and I hate this trip!"

Then he looked around at the rest of us, all of whom were still watching him. I found myself averting my eyes, noticing the two Americans were shaking nervously.

"What are you all staring at?" Marco shouted. "You know I'm right, each and every one of you. You know you only came on a trip like this to be treated like kings and queens, behaviour you would never get away with back at home where you would have to pander to some boss, or lecturer, or parent. Where being shown total respect out here means that you don't have to get your feet wet in the waters of Africa. And who would want to? Who would want to really immerse themselves in this cesspool of life? I know I wouldn't, and I've lived all over the fucking world. This place disgusts me. I can't wait to get the hell out of here."

"Then why don't you just get up and leave now."

The table all turned to me as one, and even I was surprised by my words, by how calm I sounded as I spoke.

"What?"

"Why don't you just get up from the table and go back to your room now. Why don't you just leave us alone. There are plenty of people around who have enjoyed this trip, and are enjoying this meal. Yet here you are exercising what you see as your right to lord it over everyone else. You don't have that right now, and you didn't have the right in the past. It's just your continued arrogance that feeds your insecure ego that makes you believe you do."

Hazel once again stood up for her husband. "How dare you speak to Marco like that, you don't have the right…"

"Oh shut up," Kerry interrupted. "You are as bad as he is, and just as racist. The only difference between the pair of you is that you hide behind your husband's considerable girth and let him get away with his immature tirades. You need to grow up just as much as he does. A marriage made out of European dinosaurs the pair of you."

I smiled as she said the last part, wanting to say something like 'I couldn't have put that better myself', but just then the cook marched out from the kitchen, holding a meat cleaver in his hand.

A small man with short black hair and dressed in the whites of his apron he seemed absolutely livid at being called out from his kitchen, his face barely containing his anger.

As Ilse followed him nervously, I noticed several people at the table visibly gasp.

"You!" he shouted. "Get out!"

Marco stared at him, his eyes dancing from the large horrible looking knife to the rest of us around the table and back again, whilst the crimson colour he'd been holding so long started to slowly drain from his face.

"Well!" the cook continued. "What is it going to be?"

Marco stared at the man before rising to his feet.

Even though the Scotsman towered over him the cook didn't flinch, not taking his eyes from the heavyset man as he raised his knife, more in a gesture of defiance than in an attempt to use it.

Not knowing this though, and perhaps feeling a little different about the confrontation, Marco looked around the table at the rest of us.

I found myself smiling smugly as several of the others turned their heads from him, as if finally sending the ignorant bully to Coventry where he belonged.

"Come on Hazel," he said calmly, before leaving the table, his wife following quickly behind him.

When they had finally left, the cook lowered his knife, and went back into the kitchen, his final glance towards us all we needed to see to confirm that he was still very angry indeed.

Very few of the others finished their food, the evening now ruined and over.

I though was the last to leave.

There was silence on the coach the following morning as we all drove to the airport together. Marco and Hazel had been the last to board and sat together at the front, preparing perhaps to make a quick getaway when we arrived. They didn't come down to breakfast, preferring instead to eat in their room, and said nothing to anyone else, not even Ilse the tour coordinator.

"They must be so embarrassed," Kerry whispered to me from behind my seat half way down the bus.

"Serves them right," I replied, making us both chuckle.

I sat back smiling to myself for a couple of reasons. One being that I was glad everyone had seen the pair of them for what they truly were: a couple of racist bullies, more afraid of their own shadows than of anything they might truly find out here. Secondly, that following my talk to Kerry yesterday, I had made up my mind on what I wanted to do next, and with a bit of luck everything would work out how I wanted it to.

When we pulled in to the airport, as suspected the pair of them were quick to grab their cases and head into the terminal building, not wishing anyone a fond farewell.

"Where are you going?" Kerry asked as she watched me pick up my single green bag. "Not saying goodbye?"

"Not yet," I replied. "There is something I have to do first."

Kerry considered me carefully before nodding her head. "Then make sure you do before you leave young man," she added wagging a chiding and slightly cheeky finger at me.

With a bow, I left her and Randal to organise themselves, before walking inside the terminal building. I gave myself a couple of seconds to orientate myself, taking in the crowds and the noise that I remembered so well from my arrival here, before finding the airline Information Desk I was looking for. It only took me a couple of minutes to confirm what I already suspected: that as I had booked my ticket last minute, and as it was considerably more expensive than some of the others, I could keep it open for a couple of months should I wish to as long as I paid a fee.

Using the last of the money I had on me, I paid up straight away, before ambling over to a cash point and taking out enough for the next leg of my journey.

Then I walked briskly to where Kerry and Randal were waiting in the queue to Check-In for their flight with South African Air.

"Well, this is it. I'm leaving you both here," I said excitedly.

"It was nice to meet you," Randal replied warmly, shaking my hand. "I wish you all the best for the future."

"Where are you going?" Kerry asked me, with a look of slight concern.

"I don't know yet. I'm going to head to the bus station and see where I end up from there."

She nodded to me, finally understanding, before embracing me in a hug. "Well, wherever you end up, be careful."

"I will. And thanks for the good advice. You were right about me. I was too afraid to come out here and just be myself, so I'm going to do just that. I'm going to travel around for a while and see if I can find myself along the way."

Kerry took out a piece of paper from her pocket and scribbled some words and numbers on it quickly, before stuffing it into my hand. "Here. These are my email address and phone numbers. If you need anything just yell, ok?"

"Of course," I replied, smiling warmly.

"Goodbye Karl."

"Goodbye."

The bus station was just as I remembered it: crowded with buses, crowded with people, crowded with various noises and countless smells.

I smiled to myself as I stood in the Scandinavian Buses queue, feeling more relaxed than at any time since my arrival in Lusaka and Zambia just two weeks ago. My head turned regularly as I tried to take in all the sights and sounds, as I tried to envelope all my senses in the cacophony that so stimulated me. As I looked about me, I watched as African men and women, many no older than myself boarded buses to Windhoek, Johannesburg, Nairobi and other areas throughout Africa. And I smiled as backpackers from all around the world, Japanese, Australian, Americans, jostled through the crowds in their First World attempts to reach other destinations.

I smiled because for now I was one of these people, I was free from the safety of that bubble of a package tour, and I could now breath.

"Where would you like to go?" the woman asked me from behind the counter, giving me a semi-bored look.

"Where does the next bus to leave end up?"

"Dar Es Salaam," she replied. "It will leave in 2 hours."

I smiled through the hatch at her. "I'll have a one-way ticket please."

Interlude

Email
From: Your Mother
Sent: 31st July 2008
To: Karl T

I thought you would be back by now but Busta says he hasn't heard from you as yet, and that you were supposed to contact him before coming home if you needed a lift from Heathrow.

I hope all is well and that you had a good trip and feel refreshed. Things here have been difficult. I've been suffering from nightmares now I'm alone in the house. The dreams always involve my being in my room at night knowing that your father is coming to get me and you are not there to come and save me. I always wake up sweating, but it normally passes after an hour or so.

Otherwise, I've had letters this week from both the Gas and Electric people with huge bills on them. Even though I've told them that your father was the one who needed to pay them, they are both threatening to take me to court if I don't give them the money they say is due. I will pay them, but I hope to see you in the next few days so I can show you just how useless your father actually was. I need you here now, as I have no one else to go through this with.
Finally, just a reminder that the trial is set for next week.
Your mother
Email
From: Sally Riedler
Sent: 31st July 2008
To: Karl T

Hey hun!

Ran into Busta last weekend and he said you were due back this week, so I tried your mobile phone but no answer. Are you back yet? Or are you just avoiding me?

Am away as of next weekend for a couple of weeks in Frankfurt on business, so wanted to catch up with you before I leave (if you know what I mean!). I miss the fun times we always have, so give me a call when you are back and have had a rest and let’s see if we can set something up.

Take care
S x

Email
From: autonews@willesdenherald.co.uk
Sent: 3rd August 2008
To: Karl T

Man set upon by angry mob in suspected drug attack!
A man is recovering in hospital after being set upon in the early hours of the morning by a group of up to fifteen during a violent attack last Saturday evening.

The incident took place at a party in Sudbury that the 23-year-old man was attending with his girlfriend. As he left the party at around 4am Sunday morning, the group who were harassing him for money challenged himself and his girlfriend in the street. The man, who cannot be named for legal reasons at this time, and told his girlfriend to go back into the party, and after a further heated confrontation a fight ensued and the man was stabbed several times by the group.
A police spokesman said officers are looking for a range of men aged between 18 and 30 who were seen running through the xxxxxxxxxx area of Sudbury early on the Sunday morning.
Any witnesses who may have been at the party, or who might have seen anything, are encouraged to contact Brent Police on 020-8XXX XXXX.

Email
From: autonews@willesdenherald.co.uk
Sent: 3rd August 2008
To: Karl T

First Search Area For Schools Opens
Schoolchildren were searched for deadly weapons at several schools in the borough this week in an effort to make attending the boroughs schools safer for pupils and staff. The new initiative, backed by police and MP For Brent Charles Jackson, aims to raise awareness of violent youth on youth crime by making all students pass through US style metal detectors on their way into school premises. Mr Jackson stated 'Often young people feel they need to carry weapons in order to protect themselves from others who they fear may be armed. This exercise aims to make schools a safe haven for children, and a place where once again students can concentrate on educating themselves and aiming for a better life as adults.'

PART TWO

Eight

"Look at this!" said Kato, banging the page of his paper with a hand full of slim angular fingers. "How could they vote an Indian woman as Miss Tanzania?"

"Let me see," I replied, trying to crane my head over his shoulder. "What is wrong with her? She looks attractive enough to me."

"It is not about if she is attractive Karl, it is about where she is from. And she is not from Tanzania," he fumed, pointing furiously. "Her grandparents are from India. She isn't therefore fully one of us."

I found myself feeling surprised at his comments. "Then why did they choose her?"

"Because she is lighter skinned and they think she has a better chance of winning the Miss World competition later in the year because of it."

"I don't understand…"

"Think about it, English," Kato continued, using my new nickname. "If they voted for a black woman then she would have no chance of winning that kind of competition, so they give the title to an Indian woman. It is an insult to all the beautiful black women here in this country."

"Give me that paper," replied Mary, snatching it away from us both playfully, surprising the pair of us as we didn't see her march across the room. "Now get back to work the pair of you."

"Ah, Mary," Kato pleaded. "We are supposed to be on a break."

"A break the boss said we could only have when we have finished cleaning up after lunch. We haven't yet, so you two can't read the paper. End of story."

I looked at Kato who frowned at me. "You are such a slave driver, and you always have a go at me, never Karl."

Mary stood there before the pair of us her hands on her hips, her finger wagging towards us, a stance I knew meant we were in trouble if we pushed her too far. "You know that I am talking to you both. As for being a slave driver, you love me for it. Now come on, we have work to do." And with that she threw a broom at him, which he caught deftly.

I laughed as I went back to what I was doing, clearing a number of empty beer bottles from the ledges all around the pool table on the first floor of the Miami Beach Bar in Dar Es Salaam. This was my job, I remembered smiling to myself, my thoughts returning to my past few weeks of happiness here in Dar Es Salaam.

It was a whole month since I had checked my emails.

The journey from Lusaka had been the most challenging bus ride I had ever undertaken. After paying my fee to the lady in the kiosk I went and bought myself some provisions for the journey: cakes, bottles of water and coke, crisps. Then I sat on a nearby wall and waited for my bus to pull into the right bay so I could board.

As the time approached, the crowd grew and the bus finally pulled into its stand. I walked up to the driver and his mate, a couple of plain clothed men in their early twenties who seemed more interested in loading produce and other items into the hold than they were in collecting tickets for the journey.

Eventually though, I climbed on board and took a seat half way down the crowded bus next to a shy Zambian woman who seemed nervous as she cradled her bag close on her lap. I tried smiling to her and saying hello, efforts that only elicited a shrug of the shoulders in return.

After another fifteen minutes we were on our way, right on time, and I was finally leaving Zambia.

As the bus raced out of the city and along the wide tarmac road towards the border, bouncing us along inside, one of the plain clothed drivers walked down the carriage with drinks and a cake before putting on an awful copy of a Jackie Chan video for us all to watch.

"Don't you just love the in-flight entertainment?" I remarked dryly. The woman next to me just smiled thinly before returning her gaze to the scenery as it raced past.

With a shrug, I then settled down to scenes of a hero out his natural environment, fighting to recover his memory in Namibia whilst using his strangely unforgettable Kung Fu moves on anyone who got in his way.

Over the next few hours I thought about the rest of my tour, all of who would be on their way home now whilst I was still here, this Englishman travelling alone across a continent in an attempt to find himself.

I wouldn't miss any of them, except Kerry and maybe Tanya as well. The pair of them were the only ones who seemed able to relate to me as an equal, and maybe also they were the only two who I allowed myself to be equal to as well. They talked to me like I had lived my whole life next door to them, and I related to them in the same fashion. It was only when I tried conversing with the likes of Marco and his wife that there were problems: that they saw me as less than them, and maybe I also saw them as more.

About ten hours into the journey, and after night had fallen, we were stopped at yet another Police Checkpoint: a single wooden building in the middle of nowhere, with just a few lights on to show where and what it was. Again I glanced at the woman sitting next to me, noticing her tense as she had done previously, cradling her bag even tighter to her chest.

As opposed to other stops at checkpoints so far on my trip, the policeman entered the bus, checking passports and tickets slowly as he walked along.

The Zambian woman next to me seemed to tense more and more as he approached us, and even from the corner of my eye I knew that something was bothering her about this presence of authority.

She had been nervous at all the past checkpoints but never as much as now, her eyes widening with each step the policeman made towards us, her hands almost rigid in fear around her single black bag.

The policeman stopped by us and asked for our passports or passes, and I handed him my own, the woman hesitating before taking out a blue book and giving it to him.

The policeman glanced from my passport to me then back again, before nodding returning my documents. Then he stared at the woman's own carefully, flicking the pages back and forth.

His head snapping up, he looked at her, saying a few sharp words in a language I didn't understand. With sweat beading on her brow, the woman replied quickly.

The conversation continued before the policeman asked the woman to accompany him off the bus. Excusing herself, I rose so the Zambian could get up to leave and follow the uniformed man.

"What's going on with that woman?" I asked one of the drivers as I stretched my legs outside. We had been waiting about thirty minutes, in the dead of night in the middle of nowhere.

"There is a problem with her passport, so they are interviewing her," the driver replied between puffs on a cigarette. "I suspect her papers are false so they may have to keep her here. We should be able to continue, but I don't think she will."

Sure enough, he was right. The policeman exited the hut at the side of the road after an hour and sent us on our way, but the Zambian woman didn't return.

The rest of the journey was fairly uneventful, if not downright boring, my time filled with watching the same two movies over and over, and reading snippets from the one book I had left with me that I had not read.

The only excitement came with the border crossing into Tanzania and the hundreds of men and women who were all made to disembark from whatever transport had brought them there, grab their bags, cross the border, and then resume their journey on the other side.

It was quite a few more hours into Dar Es Salaam and by the time we arrived I could have throttled the driver I was so tired. But finally we had made it to the bus station and I was free from my metal cage and its Jackie Chan torture.

I stayed the first couple of nights in the YMCA whilst trying to get my bearings, and working out what I wanted to do whilst I was here. It was all very well my deciding to come to Tanzania and wanting to find out more about Africa, its people and myself, but how was I going to do so.

I had already done all of the few sights that Dar Es Salaam had to offer. I'd visited the Askari Monument and paid my respects to all the Africans killed in World War One. I had already visited the National Museum and walked my way through the difficult history of this land, with its many different colonisers: Arab, German and British. And I had even spent some time sitting in the Azania Front Lutheran Church with its red roofed belfry, one of the most beautiful buildings in Dar.

I had laughed at the memories raised by the sight as I walked past the derelict building that was once a Woolworths, and congratulated myself on finding a city in the world that didn't have a McDonalds. I even inwardly groaned when I tracked down Barclay's Bank (even though I needed that one so I could draw out some more money).

I had done all of this. I'd had cursory conversations with several locals, but nothing of any depth, nothing that helped me to find my way in this city. I had even fought numerous guilty urges to go back home and be with my mother in her time of need.

This was my time, I kept on telling myself. This was my time to rediscover me, to recover, to reveal more about myself to myself, and I was going to do that, even if I had to stay here for a whole month before I worked out how.

It was several more boring, and frankly lonely, days before I met Julius. I was sitting by the docks one day just watching the world go by on what was turning out to be another humid day. Yet another ferry had just arrived from one of the islands and numerous men jostled for taxi fares, to carry bags, with offers of accommodation and other ways of attempting to make money.

"What are you doing here?" he asked, coming up from behind me. "I have seen you sitting here a couple of times this week."

He was a large man, older than me with a balding pate, and looked like a businessman of some sort in his white shirt, tie and slacks.

"I'm on holiday," I replied. "I'm just thinking about what I would like to do next."

He smiled as he studies me. "You are from England, am I right?"

I nodded.

"We don't see many black people from England here," he continued. "Are you staying long?"

"I haven't decided. I was thinking about trying to find a job, but that seems more difficult to do than I realised."

After telling me his name, Julius asked if he could join me, so I bade him to sit on the wall next to me. The noise from the throng before us continued unabated.

"I may be able to help you."

"How?" I asked, turning towards him.

"Well I own a bar in the city, and I am always looking for staff. Maybe you would like to work for me for a while?"

I stared at him quizzically, my defences coming up as I found myself not entirely sure if I should trust this man who I had only just met. "I don't know."

"I might even be able to find somewhere for you to stay," he added.

"Listen, I don't mean to be rude, but I don't know anything about you. How do I know this isn't some kind of con?"

Julius looked at me quizzically, before he finally understood. "Ah yes, you don't trust me. That is ok. It is very European, but it is also ok. Why don't you just think about it, and if you want to find me then I am at the Miami Beach Bar. Just ask a taxi driver for it, they all know where I am."

"Thank you. Perhaps I will come and see it this evening." I lied.

"I look forward to it." Then Julius rose to his feet and wished me well, before continuing along his way down to the docks.

That evening I didn't go to the bar, preferring instead to try and build a conversation with the Security Guard outside the YMCA, a small, squat man, who spoke little English but made every effort to help me feel welcome. It was a Saturday evening so after the last of the staff had retired for the night he turned on the television and we watched whatever was on the satellite channels. I suddenly found myself feeling tired around the time the Van Damme Double Bill started, made my excuses and went to bed to read.

As I sat in my room I remembered what Kerry had gathered about myself. At the time I was resistant to believing her, but now I realised just how right she was. I was scared. Of myself, of others, of just being out here and enjoying myself, I didn't know which one. There could have been many other reasons, but the important thing to realise was my fear of being free, my dread of that which I so desired and had taken so many steps to achieve out on this trip so far.

"I need to make more of an effort," I whispered to myself, before reaching through the mosquito net and turning off the side light.

The next day was just as boring, so in the end I took myself off to the bar Julius claimed to own. After asking a couple of the locals, I eventually found it, situated just off Samora Avenue, a small bar next to a record and video shop.

It was just after 5pm, so the place was busy with what looked like an after work crowd having a couple of drinks before going home. Tanzanian Indians and Tanzanian Blacks mingled at various tables as music played on a television screen high up in the corner. Laughing and joking they seemed relaxed in each other's company: no different to London city workers in a Wine Bar after hours I surmised.

"Jambo," I said somewhat shyly to the woman next to the bar as two men busily served from behind it.

"Hello," she replied in English, looking at me quizzically. "Can I help you?"

I ordered a beer and some peanuts and sat on one of the stools.

The woman, who was smaller than me, attractive, with black bobbed hair, wore a tight black t-shirt with the name bar on it and blue jeans. She studied me for a while longer before turning to one of the men behind the bar, who nodded twice and glanced at me, before grabbing a cold bottle of something from the fridge and placing it on the counter next to a clean glass.

"Thanks," I added, placing some money on the counter.

The woman started to reach for it.

"He doesn't pay!" came a voice from behind me.

A little surprised, I shuffled around as Julius appeared from a set of stairs next to me that seemed to lead up to another part of the bar. "This is our friend Karl. We met yesterday. Kato and Mary, I want you both to look after him."

I glanced at the woman and the man, both of whom seem to just a little suspicious of me. Then the man wiped his hands on a towel before reaching out to shake mine.

"Welcome to the Miami Beach," he said coolly.

I nodded to him as the woman said something seemingly urgent in Swahili before grabbing several beers off the bar and carrying them away to one of the tables. I also noticed the weak effort she made not to acknowledge me.

Julius then patted me on the shoulder, his beaming smile infectious. I nodded my appreciation. "You don't have to do that. I can happily pay for my own drinks."

"But I want to. Consider it my way of saying welcome. But did you think about my offer?"

"Yes I did," I replied. "When can I start?"

Nine

"You've never said why you came to Tanzania."

I looked up as Kato was busily scrubbing down one of the tables nearby.

"I told you," I replied, not taking my eyes off the section of floor I was mopping. "I'm just a tourist who decided to stay longer."

Kato frowned at me. "You are like a mystery, Karl, and Tanzanian men don't like mysteries. You live with me for two whole weeks and you say little about your life back home."

"You know all about me."

"What? That you were raised in the Caribbean, have family in London, and are an only child."

"Yes, that's it. That is all there is to tell."

Kato walked around the counter and pulled up a chair before sitting down. "Is it? I think there is more to you."

"Really?"

"Yes, I think you are looking for something."

"Why?"

"Because you are the first black man I know who has come to Tanzania to work with us."

I could feel myself frown as I stopped what I was doing. "What is wrong with that?"

"Nothing, but don't you see? That is what is so strange. We have Australians, and white British people come here all the time. The Japanese love to come to Africa, and there are many Italians that have made their homes in Tanzania. We occasionally get other European blacks, but it is very rare, and they have only ever been tourists. They come, they stay a while, and they move on. They don't spend any time with us. Yet you are."

I found myself thinking for a second before I replied. "I don't understand. Am I that unusual?"

A couple more weeks had passed and for the first time I was enjoying myself in Africa. My new job had become an important way for me to meet the locals, and many of them now referred to me 'English', knowing full well that I spoke no Swahili. They also often commented on the strangeness of my accent, my different manner, and I that didn't seem like the British black people they had heard so much about, but rarely seen.

I wasn't missing home now, nor was I lonely. I had moved out of the YMCA after Julius insisted that I reside with Kato in the flat he had given him just outside of town. Kato, who was initially hesitant about this arrangement, eventually agreed when he realised that he wouldn't have to pay out so much of his money on rent as previously.

"It means I can send more money home to my parents," he told me as we took the bus out of town one evening.

I chose not to ask him more about his comment right then because I was mesmerised by the sprawling shacks and houses I was seeing for the first time. A sea of corrugated iron or brick buildings of varying sizes and shapes. The area felt poor to me, but in some ways also more genuine.

We stopped at a set of traffic lights as we passed what looked like a rubbish tip I even saw a number of children picking their way through the refuse whilst several adults stood nearby gesticulating towards them.

"They are searching for something to eat, or to clothe themselves with," Kato said from next to me.

"How sad," I replied.

Kato just shrugged. "It is life."

I could feel my heart clench as I watched them, a feeling that stayed with me as the bus pulled away.

Eventually, we arrived at the house Julius owned. I was surprised by how much better a condition it was in than I had expected, as Kato used his key to open the door. Inside we walked along a corridor.

"There is the kitchen and television room," he said pointing swiftly to the side.

"Julius does well doesn't he?"

"Yes he does. And this isn't the only bar that he owns. He also has one in Arusha."

I nodded, not surprised anymore, as Kato showed me to the spare room: a small, sparse area, with a single light, and bed that was barely covered by a mosquito net. His room was across the hallway from mine, and there was a toilet and bathroom along the hallway.

"This is our home," Kato said proudly.

I smiled at him. "Good," I replied.

As time passed, and we got to know each other, Kato and I quickly fell into a routine of travelling into the city together: taking one of the always crowded, dubiously painted, buses into the city of Dar Es Salaam in the early afternoon. Then we would open up the bar and start getting things ready for the evening trade.

"Alright I will tell you some more about me," I replied laughing that day, leaning my mop against the wall.

"Good," Kato replied. "It is not right to be so secretive. Anyone would think you are afraid of us here. Or just of me."

"No, Kato, I'm not scared of you. I think I just grew up in a land and a culture where it became hard to trust anyone, even your neighbour."

Kato looked puzzled. "I can half understand that. It is just as difficult here in Dar Es Salaam. There are too many people here out of work. You have seen them on the streets. People will do anything to make some money. And then there are those who are willing to fight you for a job and stab you in the back. It is crazy sometimes."

"I've heard of that as well," I replied, remembering some of the emails I had read a couple of weeks back. "But it's getting worse back home. Even to go to school a child has to make sure he has a weapon, just in case he is attacked."

My friend stared at me. "What? You mean by other men?"

"No, normally other children. Something is happening back home, something strange. A friend of mine that I met in Lusaka asked me once if I was scared, and at first I found it hard to agree with her that I might be, but I am. I admit that now. I am absolutely terrified at home sometimes."

"Why?"

"Because there are gangs of children, men and women, wandering the streets looking for something dangerous to get into, and they are all scared of each other. They hustle, they fight, they stab each other needlessly, and often these are children no older than fourteen or fifteen. And the generation that is coming along fast behind them is growing up afraid of where they live, so much so that they either stay indoors playing on their computer games or join other gangs in order that they might feel some kind of security."

"That is strange to hear," Kato mused. "Yes, I am sure we have gangs here, and yes there are sometimes problems with stealing and robberies, but we are generally a peaceful people. In other parts of Africa they have that kind of violence, like in Nairobi, but here we don't like to trouble too many people too often. But I don't understand how you feel so different here."

"Because I had not realised just how tense I had become in that environment," I answered, walking over to him and sitting on a chair besides him. "If you live like a caged animal then surely you just believe you are a caged animal, even when you are set free. It then takes a while to realise that you are not a caged animal any more."

"But whilst you still believe you are a caged animal, you will always find someone to make you feel afraid."

"Exactly."

"My turn now. What do you want to know about me?"

I smiled at him. "Why do you have to do that other crazy job of yours so early in the morning? You always wake me up chasing those damned chickens in the yard."

"I do?" he replied smiling. "I'm sorry, I try to do it quietly."

"It's not you so much, it's your hens."

"Then I will tell them to keep quiet in future. I'm sure they will listen to me."

I laughed as we went back to work, getting up from my seat and resuming my mopping of the floor, whilst Kato went to collect some more bottles of beer from the basement.

Even though we both worked hard during the day, often until late into the evening, the mornings were our own to do with as we pleased.

Kato's second job, as he called it, involved him rising early each morning to collect any eggs his hens might have laid. Then he would put a couple next to the makeshift cooker before taking the rest to a local market to sell.

"It helps me make some extra money," he told me a little later a little before we opened. "It isn't much though."

"Then why do it?" I asked.

"Because I have a duty to my parents. The more I can send them, the easier it will be for them to survive."

"Are you their only child?"

"No. I have two brothers. One in Arusha, the other in Kenya somewhere, I do not know where. The last I heard he was working at one of the resorts on the coast up there."

"So your parents need the money you send them?"

"Of course. They have no other income, and my father is too old to be working in the city like myself and my brothers. They have land from which they grow enough food, but any extra money we can send them always helps to make life that little bit easier."

I found myself feeling a sense of sadness, coupled with irritation as I considered my own father.

"Don't you do the same for your parents?"

"My father is a proud man," I replied calmly. "He wouldn't accept any help at all. He wouldn't even ask, even if he was heavily in debt."

"Really? That sounds like a bad case of pride to me. Here it is expected for a man's children to help where we can."

"Well he is very stubborn. To ask for any assistance from his son might mean his is weak, and black men back home don't do weakness."

"I don't understand."

"You have to realise, Kato, my father was the type of person who wasn't easy to be around all the time. It was like walking on eggshells around him when he came home from work, and he always had this simmering air of resentment in him that seemed to almost fill the air when you were around him. If I talked to him about anything as a child he would always put me down, and any conversations we had as adults were always one sided as he continually craved victory over me.

"When I was a child he would beat me regularly, often for things I didn't actually do, or when he was just in a bad mood. And when I went to school it felt like he would bully me into doing what he wanted me to do: he never took any interest in the things I liked."

"Many fathers are like that," Kato replied.

"Maybe, but he seemed to hold some kind of pain inside of him. I could always sense that. And I never felt I truly knew him, he never spoke about himself, just about things outside of the family, or to tell me how stupid or disappointing my mother was being.

"And to cap it all, I always used to blame myself for everything, I always used to think it was my fault that he didn't relate to me as I felt a father should. I wished I'd been wiser as a child to notice that it wasn't down to me at all. Much of it was his own fault."

Kato patted me on the back as Mary entered the room. "Well maybe one day things will improve between you," he said kindly.

"I doubt it," I replied, forcing a smile.

As we continued working, I realised that as honest as our conversation was there were things I felt I still couldn't tell this new friend of mine. For example, I don't tell him about the beatings my mother suffered at his hands: the tens of years of mistreatment that all came tumbling out of their clandestine container just over a month ago. I don't tell him about my running away, my leaving for Africa, as I don't want to be there anymore. I don't tell him about my anger at him for creating this atmosphere of anxiety inside our own home, within our own castle fortress, and how that is now being replicated out there in my world, how I now carry that fear with me all the time.

I don't tell Kato, the one person here I am learning to call a friend, about the many men who refuse to father their children: whose selfishness costs their children the chance to bond with a man, the chance to test their skills against a man, to feel wanted and respected by a man, or to understand men. Or about those men who are present in the lives of their offspring, but whose children are afraid of them: after the beatings, the admonishments, the excessive chastisements that forced many a boy, becoming many a man, to fear other men, to huddle together in groups of boy/men, to hate other men, to ironically be the same men that they knew when they were just children.

I think about all these costs of insufficient parenting that I haven't the courage to tell Kato, because I am afraid, because I am ashamed, because I envy this simple African man and his cared for life.

I only exited my reverie when noticed that Mary was staring at me quizzically.

"What are the pair of you talking about this time?" she asked, placing her bag on the counter for Kato to put in the back room.

"Nothing that involves you," he replied playfully. "You are too nosey sometimes."

I found my mood lifting as Mary 'humphed' at us both, though more at him than me, as Mary still seemed to find my presence in the bar unsettling for some reason, and barely held my gaze. Instead she regularly smiled and cast her eyes downwards when she saw me, a look that puzzled me at times, especially when I was trying to be nice to her.

"We were discussing Kato's chickens and how they keep waking me up in the morning," I added finally making conversation.

I watched as she looked at me from under long eyelashes. "Well hurry up. We have to open soon," she said with a rye smile, before leaving the room.

Kato walked swiftly around the counter to come over and nudge me.

"She likes you I think."

I shook my head at him. "I don't think so. Didn't you tell me she already has a man?"

"Yes, but that is only a rumour, no one knows who he is. Even if she does, I think she has taken a liking to you, my friend."

I found myself smiling at the proposition. "Well, we will see," I replied finally.

Ten

"Mr Ali, how are you today?"

The balding, heavy set, Indian man smiled at me as he pulled up a stool. "English! It is good to see you today," he replied, slamming his palm down on the bar. "You know what I want don't you?"

"The usual?"

"Of course."

The bar had filled considerably that evening. It was a Friday, the end of the working week: the last day for these Tanzanian working men and women to come here to the Miami, as they called it, have a few drinks, and relax before the weekend began.

But tonight was especially crowded as there was a football game being played at the new National Stadium.

Tanzania versus Mozambique: another game in the long series of matches that would lead to the African Cup of Nations Finals, being held in a couple of years' time. We had already witnessed the scenes from outside the ground: men with whistles and snakes dancing to various drum beats wore green of Mozambique and the yellow of Tanzania, whilst many others sported soccer shirts bearing the names of African stars plying their trade in Europe. Drogba, Essien, Yobo, and many others bore witness in name only to the frenzied excitement gripping two nations as they contested the beautiful game.

"Hey English!" shouted Mr Shah grinning. "Have you ever seen anything like this back home?"

"Have to say I haven't," I replied. "Things are normally a lot more sedate at football matches in Britain. And even if some excitement does break out it's normally in the form of a fight of some kind."

"No fighting here boy. Just love of football on both sides. And tonight we're going to win!" Mr Ali continued, slamming his palm down on the counter again, and almost knocking over his beer.

"Your England team needs to come and play in Africa sometime," someone else added.

"Yes they do," Mr Ali added. "Why don't they come here? Do they think they are too good for us?"

"We would win easily," I replied with an easy smile.

But Mr Ali looked shocked to the core by my suggestion. "What? We would thrash them. When you go home, you must tell David Beckham that he needs to bring his team to Tanzania. Then they will know they've been in a game!"

As we all laughed, I let the conversation go on its merry way as the sun went down and the pictures from inside the attractive Chinese built stadium came through on the small television screen high up in the corner of the room.

The crowd started to quieten as the two teams came out onto the field and the national anthems were sung, with many in the bar standing to sing for Tanzania.

Then the game started.

"What should we do now?" I asked Kato seeing that things had calmed.

"There is still a lot of stock to be moved out in the back. We should make a start with that. One of the others can take care of the bar for a while."

I nodded, and Kato called over to Mary, talking to her quickly in Swahili whilst I stood by. I watched as Mary then replied, glancing at the pair of us, before picking up a cloth and walking towards us.

"We should be ok for the first half of the game at least," Kato continued finally.

"Not a football fan?" I asked him.

"Not really," he replied, wrinkling his nose. "I will watch it sometimes, but this lot will watch every match on television religiously. It is not healthy."

Outside we began cataloguing the crates of beer, making a note of what needed to be reordered, whilst stacking those of empty bottles that were due to be returned. Even though it was the evening, the humidity was still high, and it was tough work, harder than whilst we were inside in the air-conditioned environment of the Miami.

"Do you have a girlfriend?" Kato asked me after a while.

His question made me start, so I placed the crate I was holding down for a moment and wiped my brow. "What made you ask that?"

"I just think that you must have a girlfriend back home."

"Why should I?"

"The way you have ignored Mary ever since you arrived here."

I found myself laughing. "You are very persistent."

"No. I am patient. Patience is a very African thing."

"Well, I'm not sure about that. But to answer your question, yes I do have a girlfriend back in London. I have two in fact."

"Two?" Kato's eyes widened excitedly.

"Well, one and a half if you like, and try not to drop that crate."

"I won't."

"Good. I would hate for you to have to take time off with an injury. More work for me you see."

Kato grinned at me. "And already I notice how you hate hard work."

We laughed together at that, before Kato placed the last of the crates in its stack and we sat on a nearby wall to rest.

"So, who are these women in your life?" he asked me finally.

"Well," I replied hesitantly. "There is Sally, who is white, and Lilly, who is black."

"From Africa?"

"No, she is Trinidadian originally, but was born in London."

Kato nodded. "Ah I see, and what is it about this Lilly that you like?"

"I don't know," I started to reply. "She isn't really my type of person. Don't get me wrong, we have a great time when we're both relaxed with each other, and the sex is always passionate, but there is something wrong in our relationship as well. She is far too bossy and demanding for me, and she loves an argument, and will often throw things around or shout at her son for no reason. And yet I feel drawn to her. It's as if she needs me and I have to be there for her."

"That makes no sense to me."

"It doesn't to me either sometimes. I know she's had a tough life: her previous boyfriend used to beat her regularly before she finally threw him out, and her son is getting older and becoming more unruly by the day. In some ways I just feel as if I need to be there with them, as if that is my duty."

"But are you happy with her?"

I looked at him. "No. Often I'm not. There is a strong part of me that wants a quiet life: that wants to be with someone who just enjoys being with me, without all the drama, without all the chaos that comes with some relationships. Lilly though likes to always be busy: and when she isn't busy then she wants me there: and then when she's had enough of me she causes an argument or says she thinks we should split up, her complaint being that I never open up to her.

"But, there is never a time when we can just be with each other and relax. There is never a time when I feel relaxed enough to open up and tell her who I am. It is as if she is keeping things dramatic to prevent us from doing just what she wants, and blaming me for it."

"She sounds like a strange woman to me," Kato replied shaking his head.

"She is a typical black woman back home. Strong, confident, but chaotic. That is why I have Sally as well."

"This is the second one?"

"Yes, she is Scandinavian. We normally just meet up when she is in London as she travels a lot. Then we have a lot of fun together, but that is all it seems to be, just fun."

"Can you open up to her? Can you be yourself with Sally?"

"Not really."

"Why not?"

"I guess I find her a bit too cold to open up to," I replied. "I have tried in the past, but she has always rebuffed me in some say, either by changing the subject, or letting me down. So in the end I gave up trying. She is a good time girl really. Good nights out, good fun, good sex, there is nothing more to it than that. Now I think about it, it's quite sad really."

Kato studied me carefully. "Well, I've never met anyone from up there. And anyway, as you know, I prefer black African women. There are more than enough beautiful ones here for me to date without chasing European women."

"Tell me about your girlfriend then? Where is she?" I asked, smiling at him.

"Not too far from us. She lives and works at a club near to where we live."

I looked at him incredulously. "What? You never told me she was so close before."

Kato laughed at me. "You never asked. I see her most mornings when I go out to make my deliveries. Sometimes she helps me."

"And I take it when you go for your day off, you meet up with her."

"Yes."

"Cheeky," I said smiling, my head shaking. "You will have to introduce me."

"Of course," Kato replied, patting me on the back. "There is a club night on tomorrow. After we finish work we can go there if you like. You can meet her then."

"I'd like that."

"Good."

"How long have you been with her?" I asked him, giving him a wry smile.

"Since I moved to Dar," he answered. "She is a good person and we get along well. I like that we talk a lot of the time about things. About what we both want to do with our lives, where we want to live, how many children we both want to have. The usual couple stuff." There is a look in his eyes that I barely notice, or can describe: is it admiration, solace, comfort, contentment?

I found myself feeling suddenly jealous of this man as I looked at him. "That is good," I say as calmly as possible, hoping he doesn't notice my sudden, strange, discomfort.

Kato then excused himself to go to the toilet, leaving me sitting there on the wall at the back of the Miami, the bar that was my employment, my home. As the stars in the night sky rose to greet me I gave myself enough time to think through my envy of

Kato, of his relationship with his girlfriend, of the ease with which he seemed to live his life.

I felt the jealousy of man who hasn't experienced those things, those strange emotions. That contentment of knowing that a relationship is just that, a relationship; not a battleground, not a scene for constant confrontation, not a co-dependent arrangement keeping me safe from need. I realised that this man was showing me something new, that my trip to Africa was presenting me with more than I understood of relationships, of partnerships, of companionship.

Kato had been with his girlfriend here in Dar Es Salaam, worked six days a week, held down two jobs, sent money home to his parents, and survived his life, whilst I was battered and bruised by mine. I could have idolised this man if I knew how.

A roar from the full bar inside roused me, reminding me that I had work to do, that I was there for a reason, not to just sit watching the twinkling of the emergent stars.

Then, with a heavy heart, I climbed off the wall I was seated on, and drifted back inside the Miami bar.

Interlude

Email
From: Lilly Tucker
Sent: 15th August 2008
To: Karl T

Hey,
Still haven't heard from you so guessing you are still not back yet. Rang Busta last week and he didn't seem to know what was going on, but he did tell me about your mother. I'm sorry to hear your news, and hope things improve soon.
Things this end are not good for me either. Reggie got arrested last week for the first time: he is only 9 years old Karl, and I just don't know what to do. They said he was shoplifting and had been caught with some alcohol that he was smuggling out for some other boys. Reggie said that he only did it because he wanted some of his friends to like him.
Then his school report arrived. They say he hasn't been concentrating enough in class: that he spends too much time talking and messing around. When I challenged him on his report he started to get cheeky, trying to say that he did well in some of the other subjects and why can't I talk to him about those. He doesn't seem to understand that it is hard for black boys and he needs to be up there with the best if he wants to be anything in life. He deserved the beating that I gave him that night.
Then, to cap it all, last week he forgot my birthday. I don't know what to do with him, Karl, and even told him that it wasn't worth having a child for all the problems he gives me. I said to him that he was just as useless and as lazy as his father, and he will never amount to much. Of course, he just burst into tears and ran into his room, but I have no sympathy. He needs to understand.
I wish you were here to help Karl. In fact I'm angry that you are not. I need your help with Reggie now more than ever and he likes talking to you, he really listens when you sit down with him.
Come back soon…
Lilly x
PS. I miss you too.

Email
From: Busta
Sent: 21st August 2008
To: Karl T

Yes Bro!
Thought it was about time I sent you an email as I haven't heard from you since you left London (hint, hint)! What happened to you man? No one seems to have heard a peep out of you since you left, and people are starting to get worried. Spoke to Lilly some time ago and she hasn't heard anything, except that you've taken an extended leave of absence from work. Then I ran into Sally a couple of weeks ago and she said she'd emailed you a couple of times looking to hook up, but you never got back to her. Said she was getting tired of waiting on you're your sorry ass, and was really mad at you. You guys still on? If so, you had better sort things out with her soon bro as I know she's been seen out with some other brother from her workplace. I did ask her about that but she brushed me off, so be careful.
Spoke to your mother as well man, and you really need to call her soon. Did she tell you what happened at the court case? It's not good man, but I will let her give you the news. Not my place to spill the beans.
Otherwise, things here are the same. Still living in racist Britain. Maybe you saw that a brother finally won the British Grand Prix last month, and still they put a white boy all over the back page of the papers for winning some Tennis match. What does a black man have to do to get some respect? Same old Britain, same old disrespect of black people.
Anyway, let me know when you are back and we'll catch up.
Blessings…
B

Email
From: autonews@willesdenherald.co.uk
Sent: 22nd August 2008
To: Karl T

Asian Couple Complain to Police!

Mr and Mrs Kumaris from Harlesden, Brent, have complained to the police after thirty officers raided their home in the early hours of the morning last week. The officers were believed to be chasing a gunman who was thought to have gone to ground in their garden and home, but was later discovered to have fled the scene.
Mrs Kumaris said, "It was about 4am and we were sleeping, when there was a loud crash from downstairs in our shop. Then a lot of Police Officers, I don't know exactly how many, came racing up the stairs and into our bedroom. My husband asked them what they were doing, but no one said anything. They broke down our front door, and wrecked much of the shop, costing us hundreds of pounds in damages, but no one has apologised. It's a disgrace."

Brent Police refused to comment, saying they were still investigating the incident.

The gunman is still at large.

Email
From: autonews@willesdenherald.co.uk
Sent: 22nd August 2008
To: Karl T

Son of Brent MP arrested!
Nelson 'Nelly' Jackson, son of MP for Brent, Charles Jackson, was arrested this week on suspicion of being part of the gang of youths suspected of being involved in an horrific attack in Wembley: the incident that appeared in our 23rd July newspaper.

Bennie Davies, 17 years old, from Harlesden was shot in the leg in an alleged random and unprovoked attack whilst on his way home from a party. The incident brought renewed calls from within the community and local government to end the cycle of violence that was threatening to spiral out of control. Today though we can reveal that the son of our own MP for Brent, Mr Jackson, is one of the gang of youths that has been released on bail pending further investigations into the incident.

Mr Jackson, who is estranged from his son and the mother and, it has emerged, has three other children by two further partners, declined to comment on the incident, saying instead that 'the police are dealing with this matter and will in time find my son innocent of any misdemeanour'.

Eleven

I had never been to a club like it.

We were stood in what was a shack with only two sets of walls, letting in the cool night breeze and meaning that people could spread out on the ledges or the spaces outside. Electric lamps hung from hooks dotted around the shack, shedding sparse light onto the scene, whilst loud music played: African rhythms prompting the dancing that was taking place in the centre of the room.

In the far corner a group of men were busy gambling, loudly exclaiming their joy or frustration at winning or losing, whilst women in jeans and dark tops drifted through the throng holding trays of drinks.

People were laughing and talking, dancing and drinking, as I, the Englishman, sat there at the edge of it all feeling suddenly shy.

Here I was, black just like them, but only different because of displacement, trauma, colonial rule, and immigration, four small things that shouldn't have kept us apart. Yet they did. I was finding it difficult to relax in amongst these good people.

They didn't know anything about my discomfort, they didn't have to, all that mattered was that I felt a certain way, was that I felt worried I might be found out, that I should go home, that, suddenly, I was a fraud for even deciding to come here.

"What is the matter with you? You look as if you are a foreigner in a foreign land."

Kato, my host for the evening suddenly appeared with a couple of beers, handing me mine.

"Thanks," I replied. "I feel like it. This just seems to alien to me."

"You don't like it?"

"I think I love it," I said honestly. "I'm just not sure I fit in here."

Kato patted me on the back. "Don't worry, you will get used to it. It was the same for me when I first came."

"I doubt that."

"Of course it was," Kato continued. "Remember, I am not from Dar Es Salaam, and at first I didn't think I was welcome here as I come from out of town."

"Did they treat you any different?"

"Some people did back then. Now though, I've probably been coming for long enough that most of the regulars here know me, and that is enough."

"What about me then?"

My friend laughed, and slapped me on the back again, this time just a little too hard making me wince. "You will be fine as you are with me."

"I hope so," I grimaced. "Anyway, I still want to meet that girlfriend of yours you keep hiding from me."

"She is coming over right now," he replied smugly, pointing.

My head craning to scan the people in the crowd, I tried to find a first sign of this partner of my friend, suddenly spotting her, a smallish, shapely woman, who ambled over to us in an almost shy way.

"Karl," said Kato, looking both proud and a little nervous at the same time. "This is Elsie."

I shook her hand. "Nice to meet you."

"And for me," Elsie replied in a voice almost too quiet for me to hear. "Kato always speaks well of you."

"I'm glad about that," I replied politely.

"Do you like it here in Tanzania?"

"I'm enjoying my time here, yes."

"How much longer do you think you will stay?" she asked.

The question puzzled me. "I don't know. Until I get bored and decide to move on I suppose."

Elsie nodded politely.

As the music seemed to suddenly change tempo, Kato then spoke quickly to her in Swahili making her smile, before she nodded her head.

"We're going to dance," he said to me finally.

"Don't go away," Elsie added.

"I won't," I replied, only half believing myself.

For a while I watched as the pair of them danced, out there in the crowd's embrace, envious, jealous, or maybe just wishing I had the confidence to be like the pair of them.

"You've been sitting there all night."

I turned to my left to see a familiar face looking at me.

"Mary." I could feel my eyes light up just a little too much as I recognised her. I quickly tried to gather myself, regaining my composure as I took in the black, low cut, figure hugging dress she was wearing. "What brings you here?"

"Kato told me where you were going tonight, so I came with some friends."

"Well, it's nice to see you."

"And you. Not dancing?"

I smiled at her nervously. "No. I don't know this way of dancing."

"You don't dance like this at home?"

My attention turned to those moving in pairs on the wooden dance floor. "No, not that often. These days all people seem to do is dance singly, not like this. The closest thing I can match this way of dancing to is Salsa, but that is from South America."

Mary nodded as she sat down next to me. "I have seen Salsa on television. It's not that different."

"Really? You think so?" I asked, suddenly smelling her perfume.

"Yes. Why do you ask?"

"Well, I did take lessons a few years ago. Not sure if I can remember too many of the steps now though."

"Want to try and see?"

I looked over to her, noticing her smiling at me. She seemed no longer to be shy of me like she had been at work. More, interested, if that was the word I was trying to find, as if she had warmed up to me.

I couldn't refuse her offer.

We danced for most of the evening after that, and in the end I had to ask Mary for the chance to rest before she let me leave the dance floor. Then we seemed to spend a lot of time just talking. About our lives, about our families, and about what I wanted to do whilst I was here in Tanzania.

"Will you be staying?" she asked me at one point.

"I don't honestly know," I replied. "I like it here, but I'm not sure that I fit in."

Mary seemed disappointed in my answer. "Well, everyone seems to like you: Kato, the customers, even Julius, and he is a very difficult man to please."

"I just try to do a good job to repay him for his kindness," I replied. "It's not the type of work I'm used to, but I enjoy it, and he seems happy with my efforts so far."

Mary just shrugged. "Well, whatever he says, I hope you do too."

I looked over to her to see her smiling at me. "Thanks," I said finally.

It was 3am when I finally left, with Kato and his partner staying on as Elsie needed to help clean up before her shift ended.

"Let me walk you home," I suggested to Mary, who smiled and just nodded at me as we walked out of the club.

"I don't live far from here," she told me once we were outside. "And it should be easy for you to get home afterwards."

"Well, I've spent enough time walking around here by now to know some of the routes in and out of this place."

"Sounds like you are getting used to living here."

I laughed. "Yes, I suppose I must be. What about you? Are you from Dar?"

"No, I moved here from Kitwe three years ago, after my father died."

Stopping in the street I looked down at her, suddenly feeling a sense of sadness. "I'm sorry to hear that."

Mary touched me on the arm softly. "Don't be, he was a good man, he was good to me, and I loved him. Our problems started though after he left as we had no one to provide for us, my mother and I, and I don't have any brothers. There are no jobs in places like Kitwe for women, so my only chance was to either get an education or find work. In the end I chose to move here."

I nodded. "So what are you hoping to do?"

"Right now I am saving as much money as I can. Then maybe in the future I can go to school and study. I want to do more with my life than just work in a bar."

"Good," I replied.

"Good?" Mary seemed shocked by my response. "You don't mind that I want to work and have my own money?"

"Why should I?" I replied. "Back home, most women work or at least have the opportunity to do so. My mother worked for forty years before she retired. I'm not saying it was easy for her, there were other obstacles, but she did the best she could. Without her efforts I would never have had the chances I did."

"Then she is very lucky. It is hard for women here to make it through school, even if the government talks about wanting us to be better educated."

We talked for a short time longer, but after only five minutes Mary stopped me and we were stood outside her place, a small nondescript house slightly larger than the one myself and Kato shared.

"You live here alone?" I asked.

"No, with my mother. She came with me to Dar after my father died."

"Isn't she lonely here without her friends from home?"

Mary hesitated before answering, and in that moment seemed just a little uncomfortable with my question.

"Did I say something wrong?"

"No you didn't," she replied quickly. "She is happy enough here. My mother likes her own company a lot of the time, but when she wants too there are some people nearby who she visits."

"Good, I'm glad she has company here."

Mary looked up at me smiling.

"What?" I asked, feeling a little uncomfortable under the spotlight of her gaze.

"You are a strange man, Karl."

"Why do you say that?"

"You are not like Tanzanian men. You are kind and thoughtful, and you ask questions about me and who I am and what I like. You don't assume for me. And, most of all, you are the first foreign man I've ever met who wasn't staying just a night on his way home to America or Europe."

Not sure what she meant by all that, I could feel my brow furrow. "Am I really that strange?"

"I don't mean it in a bad way," Mary replied smiling, as she again touched my arm to reassure me. "I mean you are not what I am used to. I sometimes think the men here don't care about women in the way you do. Often they just think about one thing, and don't even wonder if a woman is worth anything more than that."

"Well, I think that is men all over the world to be honest," I laughed. "They all often just think about sex. I'm sure I can be the same sometimes."

"Maybe you can, you are only a man after all."

"Thanks."

"But you are also more than that. You have a respect for women I'm not used to. I saw it in the way you danced with me. You seemed a little uncomfortable leading me, as if to do so was wrong, and that interested me."

"Well, it was a challenge to me at first," I admitted. "We don't dance that way that often back home, normally on our own as an individual with another individual. Here it was more about being a couple."

"And it felt to me as if you found that challenging."

"I do sometimes. It's as if I'm not always allowed to lead back home, in more ways than one. It's as if to be a black man I have to separate out from someone, to be an unconnected entity, and that any type of control is frowned upon. So I don't often know if it is alright for me to be masculine and take the lead at times, or if it will be seen as an attempt to belittle or dictate to.

"Here, for the first time in an age, it became acceptable for me to just lead. I could take charge of a situation, yet with an understanding that there was another person there I needed to be respectful of, and that was a surprise for me."

"And if you had not been respectful to your partner, she would not have let you walk her home," Mary added coyly.

"Exactly."

"Then I am glad we are on the right page," she continued, before standing on her toes in order to give me a quick kiss on the lips.

"I think we are," I replied with just a little embarrassment.

Mary returned my gaze before she excused herself and sauntered casually up to the door of her house. Then she turned once, waved to me, and went inside.

It was a few moments longer before I departed, wishing as I was perhaps for her to return to me, to come back outside so we could talk some more, but also careful and happy that she hadn't done so.

As I walked back home through the streets I pondered what it was about Mary that left me feeling so elated. Was it her? Or what it something that she represented?

I loved being able to lead, I realised. I loved being able to dance with her in a way that meant I was in control, that she felt able to acknowledge me as a man. Something that was alien to my world back home in Britain, where I had become used to being brought in to discipline like by Lilly: to save, as my mother would do: or just to fuck, like Sally so often enjoyed.

There was no sense of my being acknowledged as a man, not even by my father, the man of the house, the man who I was supposed to receive my guidance from.

They all undermined me. Mother, Sally, Lilly and my father, they all used their own ways to put me down, to take me apart, to leave me less than. And I let them. I let Sally disappear when I needed her to be more than just a fuck buddy, and always took her back. I let Lilly cause the numerous arguments that I would always lose as she would never acknowledge her role in them. I let my father put me down, sabotage my schooling, and tell me I was worthless and believed it was my fault in order that he might love me. And I let my mother beat me to keep me tied to her, her protector, her warrior against the hordes of Hades, the world of men.

"There are no good black men out there!"

I would hear that regularly at the bus stop, in work, in clubs, wherever I was, no woman would acknowledge the worth of a man. Yet if a man commented on a woman in this manner then he would probably be considered sexist, or worse.

"All women are slappers!"

Such powerful phrases, such powerful put downs. Designed not to bring together, but to divide apart. But what they don't acknowledge, I realised as I walked, is the pain of hearing phrases like that.

"How much pain?" I asked myself.

How much pain do we need to put ourselves through with comments designated to destroy confidence, not to build it. What must it be like for a boy to hear his mother utter that phrase in his presence? What must it be like for a man to hear that comment from the woman he loves? What does it say about her true feelings about him?

What must it be like to have these comments uttered time and time again, from Pastor to Lawyer, from Grandmother to Grandchild, how destructive you bastards are, and you don't even realise it.

"And I've probably said these same phrases myself," I mused as I approached my front door. "I let them all emasculate me, because that is what we do."

Twelve

It was with exasperation that I read my emails around a week later. Exasperation and exhaustion, a tiredness that I hadn't ever noticed in myself before, a weariness that washed over me, wrenching from me freedom's first flickering after my kiss with Mary.

Generally, after that night, I had felt noticeably more relaxed than when I first arrived in Africa. I was smiling a lot of the time, and didn't feel tired or bored of my job.

Julius, who had just returned from a business trip to Kenya, noticed my good frame of mine, as did some of the customers. Even Kato saw that I had a different feel to me than before.

"You look as if you have won the lottery," he commented, patting me on the back as we worked a shift. "Don't forget to share your winnings with your friends."

"This one I can't share," I replied.

"Well, you can at least tell me all about it later, otherwise I will begin to think you are ill."

But it was Mary who brought the most light into my life. We barely said anything more to each other whilst we worked, but would often find time to take our breaks together, allowing us small stolen chances to talk and just take stock of where we were with each other.

There were differences to how we interacted as well. Like, after our evening at the bar, she seemed to revert back to how she had been before in some ways, being more reserved in the company of others, but when we were alone she would become markedly more open, telling me as much as she could about her life, as I did the same.

In some ways, I felt as if I could have been a teenager again: enjoying the stolen instants of intimacy, revelling in the secret glances and gestures that marked us out as a possible couple.

It was as if I had set myself free from the restrictions of how I was supposed to be back home, where my responsibilities were many, and my nonconformity nonexistent. I could be me here, with no mother and father to worry about, no job to be concerned for, and no girlfriends putting pressure on me.

I enjoyed those few days of freedom, but like a Prison Officer walking towards me with the keys to my cell, those emails just led me straight back into jail again.

"Tell us about this Busta," Julius asked as we sat down one Saturday, taking a well-deserved break between the lunchtime and the evening shift. I was sitting with my boss and Kato as we ate a simple meal of fish and rice together, whilst Mary finished wiping down some of the glasses behind the bar. "What is it about him that makes you so depressed?"

I found myself unsure of just where to begin as I finished a mouthful of food. "Well, for example, I'm sick of the way he thinks."

Kato sat back and started at me, a puzzled look on his face. "What do you mean?"

"In his email he writes about that black Racing Driver, Hamilton. Do you know him?"

"I've heard of him, yes," Julius replied.

Kato also nodded.

"Well, whenever something goes well for a black man, it's as if he expects the British press to celebrate it in its totality, excluding any other type of sports news. Then when they don't give a black man his due, he claims the press are racist and not to be trusted."

"But what is the problem with that?" Kato asked. "The newspapers are often biased against people."

"I agree, but everyone has some type of bias within them. When Hamilton first started racing in Formula 1, Busta was the first one to tell people that he wouldn't win because he was black, or that because of his colour, the other drivers wouldn't respect him. There is always a reason with him why black people can't succeed, and it is never to do with themselves. Or that he wasn't actually black at all but Mixed Race and therefore not one of 'us'. It's as if he himself can never see the positives, or celebrate them when they come around, he has to put them down."

"That is a very narrow way to think about the world," Julius suggested.

"I agree, but this is the way a lot of my friend think back home. They believe they live in a racist environment, that Britain is always against black people, and because of this that we will never be accepted as one of them."

Kato seemed a little puzzled by this. "Is that true?"

"He has a point Kato, but sometimes I think we expect too much from the British, as if they owe us something. My father once said to me that he remembered a time back in the 1960s when we were so excluded that some of the political parties even ran slogans saying 'If you want a nigger neighbour vote Labour'."

"That sounds quite horrific," Julius said, his nose wrinkling.

"I can't imagine what it must have been like for them back then, but even though things have moved on, I wonder if we expect too much from the British. And we can be extremely prejudiced ourselves."

"What do you mean?"

"Well, towards homosexuals and lesbians for example."

Kato shifted uncomfortably on his stool.

"Well, I have a different view. I often wonder how a culture that has such a distorted view of sexuality in the first place can have any opinion on homosexuality at all. How in the world can we claim to be victims of injustice when we're the first ones to oppress members of our own race? It makes no sense to me."

"But homosexuality is wrong," Kato mumbled.

I looked at him, watching him for a while. He seemed very nervous about the route this conversation was taking. "How?" I replied finally, challenging him.

"Because the Bible says it is," he continued. "They spread disease, the gays. They are disgusting people, who should be shot on sight. We don't tolerate them here in Africa and quite rightly so."

I wanted to say something more, but it was Julius who came to my rescue. "It is wrong in the Bible because someone has decided as much, not because it is exactly so. There is much in the Bible that could be suggested as wrong but that isn't. In many ways the fact people hang onto their religion so much is the reason behind many of the wars and conflicts we have in the world today.

"And," he added. "How right is it to persecute someone for being different. I have to admit, my cousin in Kenya is Gay."

Kato stared at him shocked.

"Ah, it is nothing new. Our family knew about this from the moment he was born. But he has had a terrible life. When he went to Uganda the people there quickly suspected what he was, even though he had never actually said or done anything with anyone, and still they hounded him out of the country. My cousin said that he was glad to leave with his life, and that he would never go back there."

I thought about what Julius was suggesting, seeing the obvious similarities in my own Caribbean culture, puzzled by how a culture that could claim to be so persecuted like my own could then do the same to another minority group within it. Leaving it hidden, suppressed, and fearful of the majority. I felt my anger rise at the hypocrisy of it all, of the narrow-mindedness of views held, and the internalisation of our abused past.

Kato though just stood beside me and shrugged, choosing to say nothing more on the subject, but I could see that he didn't like the point we had both made. "Anyway Karl, what else does your friend say?"

"Well," I continued. "He also mentions Barack Obama,"

"Hmmm," Julius mused. "He is an interesting man that one."

"I agree, but Busta is so negative about being black. He believes deep down that Barack Obama will never win the election to become President of the United States of America as he is a black man. When he was running against Hillary Clinton he didn't think Obama would last through the first few Primary Elections."

"It must have been a real surprise to him when Obama won for his party," Julius surmised.

"I don't know," I replied. "He hasn't written to me about it since, which is no surprise really because then he would have to admit that he was wrong. And that is something that Busta could never do, because he is too proud to admit his faults, we all are. If we had any courage at all we would be able to stand up and say that the biggest obstacle to us achieving our goals in this world is actually ourselves."

Mary, who had by this time stopped her cleaning, came to join us, pulling up another stool from nearby. "I don't understand what you mean."

"Well look at it this way. The two biggest controversies in Obama's election path so far, what were they?"

The three of them just stared at me, before shaking their heads.

"The Pastor from Obama's own church, and that dumb Rap song released on a mix tape during the summer."

"Ah," Kato said. "Yes, I heard about these."

"Good," I replied. "But look at them both. Where have they come from? From within his own community. First of all his own Pastor, a man who was in many ways like a father figure to Obama can't keep his mouth shut and stay out of the limelight, letting his 'son' get on with the work on the path he has set himself. No, he decides to stand up and create a lot of confusion around him, undermining Obama just as he was threatening to put his opponent out of contention, thereby bringing her back into the game.

"And as for that song. All that rapper did was to remind people of just how afraid they are of Black people: with the song's posturing, misogynistic lyrics, sounding as if he was telling an already nervous Hispanic, White, and Afro-American public that black people were about to take over the world."

"He must have been an idiot to do that," Kato added.

"I agree, but this is the point. Even prominent black activists have come out to insult Obama, not seeing the positives that have arisen out of all of this. I was reading on the internet that McCain now has a female Vice Presidential nominee, a Palin woman. And as I was reading about her views, about her right wing politics, I felt really scared. I felt frightened that we might have another four years of Bush era style politics, filled with war and scandal. When I saw McCain's cynical appointment, and read about the brief 'bounce' in the Opinion Polls, I realised just how desperate some people are when they smell power."

"I read about her as well," added Julius. "But she doesn't have any real experience. So isn't that important?"

"I hope so. I hope the populace see just how dangerous a woman like that might be. Yet, with the negative projections that black Americans are sending out the rest of that nation might still decide Obama is too big a risk." I stopped what I was doing for a second, feeling my frustration rising before continuing. "Look, even if he doesn't win, even if Barack Obama doesn't make it to the pinnacle that is the President of the United States of America, he will have done so much to show black people across the Western World that they can be that bit more. From Gen Powell to Condolessa Rice, to Obama, they have shown that if you are good enough you will get there. All this stuff about black people being victims and never amounting to much is now just bullshit."

As Mary put her hand to her mouth, I realised just what I had said, and just how passionate I had become about this subject. Even Kato was shocked by the strength of my argument, though he just turned to look away nervously, whilst Julius burst out laughing, before slapping me hard on the back.

"Then, maybe there need to be more people like you out there," he said smiling. "This is not a problem we've had here in Africa. The majority of our leaders are black, and lots of black people work in positions of power here, this is nothing new to us."

"So I've noticed, even by watching the crowd of people that come in here. And in some ways even that surprises me. We see so much about Africa at home, so much that is negative: we hear about the corruption, the dictators, and the wars, but we don't get to see the positive face of political Africa. We're not introduced to the blacks in positions of power, we're not presented the numerous black leaders of black countries, and we hear little of the female leaders that work alongside the men across the continent. We don't even get to see the black faces on the billboards across cities like this one."

"You are really very passionate about all this," Julius said smiling. "But have you taken all of this personally? It is not about you, you know."

Sitting back in my chair, I gave myself a second to think, eating a mouthful of my now cold food, before wiping my mouth. "I think it's the victim mentality I find so difficult to handle," I replied. "It's so ingrained in us back home. Yes, we were that, yes we have been it for so many, many years, but we're not that now. Yet we try so hard to stay in that role, to play the injured party, the sufferer, the wounded. It's like we embrace it and revel in that post, that position: as if to even consider being something else, something more, would take us out of our comfort zone. And that might scare us to death."

"But what about you, Karl?" We all turned as Mary spoke. "You are just like them in many ways, I see it in your eyes. You are just the same."

As I stared at her she continued.

"I remembered how you were at the dance. You seemed nervous, scared to express yourself, reserved even. As if you had to be a certain way. Yet, it didn't suit you. When I saw you there sitting by the wall, I hesitated to come over and talk to you at first."

"Why?" I asked, not sure that I really wanted to know.

"Because you seemed petrified. You seemed scared of all of us having fun, dancing, and just enjoying life in our own way. It was if you had brought your British clothes with you here to Tanzania, and they didn't fit you any longer, but you still had to wear them because you didn't have anything else to put on."

"That is an interesting point," Julius added. "I noticed something similar when we first met and I offered you a job. You we're nervous about how to talk to me, maybe because you weren't sure about me as an African and you as British. Perhaps you thought you had to be like our own colonial masters with me, I don't know. I'm just glad you relaxed in time."

"Thanks," I replied wryly. "I think."

"But there is a point here," Kato added, obviously thinking things through as he spoke. "London is where you are from, Britain is where you were born, so it would make sense that you would be like them in many ways. If you really hate to be that victim, then what part of you actually hates yourself?"

I sat back and looked at them all individually, my mind racing, fighting for some other solution to replace that growing sense that Kato might be right. Maybe I had just grown to be more than my peers in Harlesden: perhaps I was more enlightened after my time working in East Africa. So could I conceivably now be more than my black brothers and sisters just because I'd set foot back in the Motherland?

Thirteen

The sun was setting as we both sat there, overlooking the busy bay where the last of the evening's ferries was about to depart: carrying tourists and families across to the predominantly Muslim island of Zanzibar. We watched as colourful women dragged playful children behind them, and as tourists, dressed always in shorts, shifted uncomfortably in the heat of that late afternoon. Men in jackets and shirts, obviously going home from conducting business elsewhere, sat calmly in the sun, and porters hoisted tables, chairs, and large suitcases over their heads, creating a cacophony of noise whilst they waded through the crowd.

As we watched the scene, I took a sip from the bottle of lemonade and glanced over at Mary as she did the same. Catching me staring at her, she smiled and shook her head.

"What is it?"

"Nothing," I replied. "I'm just enjoying spending some time with you."

Mary put her hand on mine, softly touching me before removing it. "Well, don't get too comfortable, we have to go back to work tomorrow."

"Thanks for reminding me," I replied.

It was a Sunday, a few days after that major conversation during our break at the Miami, and Mary had cajoled me into stealing a little time with each other, safely hidden from our place of work.

We had spent most of that weekend together, be it at work or otherwise. After another long week at the Miami, Mary took me back to the club, and we had danced together for most of the evening.

It was different that time. I felt more challenged as I led her around the floor. Challenged by her words to me the other night, experimenting with being more fearless, with finding that fire I knew was somewhere within me, with tearing off the ill fitting suit I was still wearing.

All that happened though was I made more mistakes. I tripped on occasion: stood on her toe on another: and generally made more of a buffoon of myself than I wanted to. I know Mary noticed: it was in her dark brown eyes. I was grateful for her kindness in not telling me so.

That evening was also the first time we made love. She stayed with me in my little room whilst Kato, my eternally untidy flatmate I was discovering, was away. There was a tenderness to the way that I touched her, and a shyness in the way she found me. As we both stood there naked in the moonlight of my room, I found myself wanting to do something I had never done with a woman, letting my hands drift over her shoulders, neck and back. Turning her around so my fingers could trace the grooves of her skin over her back, buttocks and down her inner thighs.

I kissed her softly on the backs of her calves, and turned her around, planting delicate butterfly kisses up her body slowly, her thighs, stomach, breasts, and neck. Kisses that led me all the way up her form until we were face to face once more.

Mary was shy of me. I could tell that, as obviously excited she tried to do the same, grasping me tenderly but tentatively, her fingers wanting but resisting their search of her mate. Digits that fidgeted, fussing nervously over my body until I stopped her, taking her hands and kissing them to say thank you, before leading her to the bed.

We made love that night tenderly. I wore a condom even though she didn't say I should, as Mary looked at me with a combination of indignant shock and pleasant surprise. The contrast noted for later we still embraced each other in kisses and caresses as we coupled, as she made me orgasm from underneath me.

With the following day being one of rest, it felt right that we take a trip to the beach in the morning, that I hire a taxi to take us both there: a friend of hers who gave me a good price on driving us around for the day as he wouldn't normally be working.

Then I took her for lunch in one of the bars up the coast, frequented more by tourists and ex-pats than locals, before her friend brought us back to the seafront in downtown Dar.

"Have you ever travelled?" I asked her.

"No," she replied. "Not to a far away place as you have."

I turned to look at her. "I've travelled far have I?"

"Compared to me, you have."

"In some ways I don't think I've come very far at all."

"Why do you say that about yourself?"

I felt myself shrug. "Well, I have so much to learn about myself, and about my world. As I sit her watching all of this noise, I feel as if I know nothing about this place, nothing about myself before I arrived here. Everything I thought I knew before was a fallacy, was fake. As if it was put there in order to stop me being me."

Mary looked at me and shook her head, before turning away. "Sometimes I think you are too serious Karl," she replied. "You need to trust yourself, that is all I think you need to do. You need to realise that you are a good person and trust that part of yourself. And that this part will connect you to the other parts of you that you are looking for."

"I find that so hard to do," I countered.

We sat there in silence. Not for long, just for enough time to watch the latest ferry to Zanzibar shuffle away from the dock, before picking up speed and racing out to the straits.

"I would like to go there someday," I mused finally.

"I trust you, Karl."

"What?" I could feel my shock as Mary said those words. "Why would you trust me? You don't even know me."

"You don't have to know someone totally to trust them. I trust you because you are kind to me, because you care. I trust you because when I spent time with you last night you were tender with me, not rough and coarse, and you loved me like no man I've ever known has loved me before.

"You are worthy of my trust because the men I normally know here don't know how to do the things you did with me last night. You cared about me as we made love, and you used protection, something that most men here consider an affront to their masculinity. You took control of me as I gave myself to you, and I appreciated that."

"Thank you," I said when she had finished, looking at her.

"My pleasure," Mary said in return, and again she did that thing where she placed her hand on mine tenderly, just for a second so I knew it was there, before removing it.

Again the blast of sound from the waterfront assaulted our senses as the throng of barely clothed men jostled and joked amongst themselves. I smiled as I watched them, frightened by the heavy work they were doing, in poor conditions, with no support for their backs, or their clothes. Driven on only by the need to survive, to make money, to eat food.

"The Health and Safety Executive would cum in its pants if it saw this lot," I mused to myself.

"What did you say?"

"Oh nothing," I replied smiling.

"Hmm. Tell me about your partner back home. You must have someone."

"Why must I?"

"Because you are a man, and you are single and have no children. I am surprised that no woman has made you get married, or that your mother hasn't selected a wife for you."

I found myself laughing at that last comment.

"It is not as easy as that where I come from," I retorted. "Almost anywhere else in the world, if a man is single and eligible then maybe he would find himself courted by women, but I've never felt as if I was wanted in that way."

"I don't understand. Then how were you wanted?"

"There is one woman that I used to see back home," I began with a sigh, my lie including deciding to leave out Sally for now. "Her name is Lilly. She's a bit younger than me, and has a son who is nearly ten by now. I worked with her, which is how we met. She didn't like me at first, said I was too quiet, too shy for her, and too nice as well."

"That is strange, that someone can be seen as too nice."

"Yes, I agree, although it depends on why they are being nice I suppose. I was the sort of person who was nice because I was taught to be that way, but I've also met people who are nice and good to people because they want others to like them, and that can seem a little bit creepy."

"I know what you mean," Mary added. "It is as if they are not confident within themselves."

"Exactly. Anyway, at first Lilly didn't like me, then when she heard that I was seeing someone else, she made every effort to make me interested in her."

Mary laughed. "That is typical of some woman. Sometimes we always want what we cannot have. Then when we get it we don't want it anymore."

I stared at her, an obviously worried look on her face. "I hope you're not like that."

"Not at all. You can have me without a doubt," again the pat on the back of my hand.

"I'm glad," I replied smiling. "Anyway, eventually I agreed to go out with Lilly, so we met for coffee a couple of times, then went to see the occasional movie. In the end, I left my girlfriend and we started dating."

"And then things started going wrong?"

"How did you guess?" I replied, chuckling. "From the moment I committed myself to Lilly she caused me problems. From accusing me of seeing other women, to wanting to check my phone whilst we were out: from causing arguments in public places, to going through my email account and sending messages to women I haven't spoken to in years. She has caused me problem after problem since I've known her."

"Then why stay with her?" Mary asked, as the horn went of the next ferry coming into port, the sound generating a rush of action on the quayside as porters and officials raced back and forth readying themselves to make more money.

We watched for a while in silence, the time giving me space to think and formulate my answer. "Because of her son, Reggie I suppose," I replied. "He is a good lad and his father is useless. We've always gotten on well, occasionally spending days going out together, be it to watch football, or see a movie: we would call them our 'Boys Days' where we would leave his mother at home and just hang out somewhere. If I'm honest, sometimes I used to think his mother treated him badly to make up for the fact she was angry at his father: he used to beat her when they were together. Some of the fights Lilly and Reggie had were horrible to witness, so I would often excuse myself and go home. They were just so painful to watch.

"It is as if she can't hold the shame of having met and married so useless a man in the past that she takes it out on her son, binding him to her. As if her pride and anger won't let her access the pain and sadness of repeating some pattern of her own. As if to trust someone new would be just too difficult, so she created with me the perfect storm, arguments on arguments, separation upon separation. One minute we are on because she needs me, the next we are off because she says I'm too nice or too good for her."

As the evening ferry came to a noisy halt, I noticed Mary staring at me. She seemed to be almost reading me, her gaze leaving me feeling a little shy. "You never knew where you were with her, did you?"

"No, I didn't. I suppose I chose her for similar reasons looking back on it. I too have had many opportunities to walk away, to leave her and find someone who would want me. Damn it, I even had the opportunity to go back to my ex-girlfriend (and one time she asked me to marry her), but didn't take that one up because for some stupid reason I felt I needed to make a go of things with Lilly and Reggie."

As I spoke about my past relationship, and as the new revelations about my inability to trust others and myself flowed up to the surface, I sat back and took another sip from my drink, before placing the now flat lemonade on wall beside me.

To just think about my relationships in this way, to consider the many routes I've taken, shocked me. It was as if I was a pinball bouncing myself away from one commitment or another, using Sally when I needed to feel powerful and replace Lilly, yet I was never obliged to her: and using Lilly when I wanted to feel connected to a family yet never be constrained by it.

I was as untrustworthy as they were, as avoidant as they were, as hesitant and living a life of safety in numbers as they did. I just never had the courage to sit down on a wall somewhere foreign, whilst sharing a drink with someone I liked, and actually see it that way.

As we watched the world go by, as we maintained that intimate space within the busiest of environments, I felt for the first time as if I wanted to try again. I wanted to be with someone, to be exclusive, to try and just enjoy myself with herself, to attempt to build something real for a change.

But could I trust myself?

Could I trust myself to make the right choice in a person, to not throw myself into something that might break my heart? And just where did this inability to trust rise from in the first place? It couldn't have come from just nowhere, could it? I can't have been born with an inability to trust? With an incapability to know just who was right and who was wrong to trust: without that invaluable radar that might lead me to have faith in others.

As I sat there I realised just how much I had to learn about trusting others and myself. I felt that right now, as I was sat on that wall, and as the final ship of the day docked with its cargo disembarking, it was time to tell the woman next to me just how I actually felt about her.

"I suppose I've been just as avoidant of her as she has been of me," I said with as much calm as I could muster. "I've been the abused to fit in with her abuser. I've been the victim of our relationship in the past, like she was the victim in hers. And I've never believed in, or trusted myself to have anything different. Until now maybe."

Mary seemed a little surprised by my words, surprised and embarrassed. "Are you sure?"

It was my turn to place my hand on top of hers, this time for a little bit longer. "Of course. I like how you make me feel, and I've really enjoyed being out with you today. I feel I can trust you, and you respect me, and there is none of the game playing that can go on in other relationships I've had. If I'm going to make a go of things here in Tanzania, that involves meeting people and maybe even settling down, and I think I would like to try and do that with you."

"But you know nothing about me," Mary countered. "I've asked about you, and you've been very honest, so I appreciate that, but I have a past as well, and would need for you to accept that if we were going to be together in any way."

I could feel myself closing down slightly, as if the trust I was trying to engender here wasn't about to be reciprocated and I needed to defend myself. The pull to be my older self, my avoidant self, it was almost too seductive for me to resist. "What do you mean?"

Mary glanced away, looking out to the sea beyond us as angry clouds started to drift in from the East. "It's going to rain," she said softly.

"Darling, tell me. What do you mean?"

She turned back to me before she spoke, the pain in her voice audible. "We all have a past Karl, and I have one too. I was in love once, with a man back home."

"I can understand that," I replied calmly, trying to make her feel she could trust me, whilst also fighting that childlike urge to run away right there and then. "What happened to him?"

"He…," she hesitated. "He left me for another woman." Again she turned from me, sitting stiffly, her back straight, as if not wanting to take the conversation any further.

Yet still I wanted to know more.

"Do you still miss him?"

"No. I hate him for what he did to me. He was older than me, a lot older. He didn't know how to treat me like you do, and I was too young to want more from him."

"Then why do you sound so angry at him still?"

"I don't know. Maybe it is because he was the first man I ever loved, and to meet a man, to fall for him that first time, then to have your heart broken is the hardest thing in the world."

"I think I understand."

She stared at me, her deep brown eyes welling up with tears. "Do you, Karl? Can you really know what it is like to have someone you love break your heart in such a way?"

"I think so, yes," I replied, not totally convincingly.

"Then maybe you are the type of man I need in my life right now. The type of man who can help me to trust again."

"Much like you are doing for me."

"……. like we are doing for each other," she countered.

I smiled at her then. Smiled broadly, warmly, as the sun disappeared and the angry clouds released their heavy drops of rain onto us and the docks. And as the storm broke, the rain covered the few tears that had started to roll free from Mary's eyes, hiding the emotion she had begun to show.

Taking her face in my hands, I then kissed her. Once, softly on the lips, prompting her to place her hands on mine and kiss me back. Then we jumped down off that wall, and ran with the crowd of men and women racing for cover, before I finally hailed our taxi, asking our driver to take us home.

Fourteen

"Come on. Julius doesn't like it when we're late."

"I'm moving as fast as I can."

"Then move faster!"

I smiled as Kato ran out of the room, towel still wrapped around his waist, clean white shirt still on its hanger in his hand.

As I sat there on my bed, cleaning the pair of good shoes I could find from the many street sellers and hawkers down town, I noticed my amusement at my friend's fussiness. We were both getting dressed for a special event Julius was hosting at his home across the other side of town, a dinner party for numerous members of the government and other important businessmen and women.

Weeks had passed since that Sunday with Mary and we were still together, seeing each other almost every day at work, and squeezing in more intimate moments when we could. I was finally happy, and only occasionally missed home. I had not checked my emails for a while, not wanting to hear the 'news'.

Dabbing more shoe polish onto the cloth I had acquired from somewhere, I continued rubbing my shoes, continuing to bring them up to a shine.

"Just like my father used to do."

The words exited my mouth before I had a chance to realise I was saying them, reminding me about him now, and about him when I was a child.

He would do exactly this, I recalled. On those rare days when we all went out as a family, he would sit as I was: trousers on with braces hanging low, shirt ironed and ready nearby, shoes in his hand as he polished them. This was his way of presenting himself to the world, of readying himself for his friends. This was the ritual he would perform, the practice passed onto me.

I wasn't surprised that he hadn't tried to contact me since I had been away, and I was in no way shocked by the failure of my friends to even mention him in their correspondence. Least of all, it didn't astonish me that I thought about him so rarely.

My father was a loner, a man who enjoyed his own company, who was happier behind a copy of the Sporting Life, than he might have been bouncing his child on his knee whilst reading Whizzer and Chips. He was an extremity, an addition to myself and my mother. The rod she brought in to discipline, not a parent to be devoted to. He might as well have stood in the corner of the bedroom awaiting that next command to punish, his presence was so lacking.

"No!" I said sharply, banging the shoe down on my lap, causing myself considerable pain as I did so. "That's not fair."

Yet it was.

That was the role he played, and the role he took on now. I had no idea where he was after his separation from my mother's side, and I suspected that he enjoyed that. The distance, the silence, the being left to his own devices whilst he betted away his pension, they all probably gave him what he wanted, his ideal position in the world. He could be the distant black father and not worry about it. In being that man who his son didn't see, who his wife didn't care about, but who had provided a child to the world: he had done his bit, his penis had played its part, and he needed to do no more.

He could sit in his one room, a retired old man, a sad betting addict, and just play the odds to his hearts content. The only emotions he needed to feel were those generated when the horse he had backed either won or lost.

I was surprised by how angry at him I was, but was all the anger mine. Yet I asked myself, was I angry at him from before I was born? Did I collect the anger that was my mother's and just hold it for her, taking responsibility for her feelings as a way of making her love me?

Or was I genuinely angry at him? Did his distance from me pain me? Did his punishments of me make me feel ashamed of myself, as if I was unlovable? Did my fear of him mean I could never be angry to his face, or even behind his back, leaving me no other option but to be angry at the world around me?

"Hurry up!" shouted Kato again, who was stood in my doorway, his black suit on, his eyes looking at me urgently.

My musings shattered, I just shrugged my shoulders at Kato and put on my shoes, before quickly finished dressing, before I grabbed my jacket so we could leave.

The journey to Julius' place took no more than twenty minutes and was in a better part of Dar Es Salaam just to the North of the city. His house was located on the beach, in an area situated alongside those purchased by a mixture of the Tanzanian and African elite, and expatriates from Europe.

As the guard closed the gate behind us to the walled compound, I immediately felt a sense of dread about the evening ahead.

Since I had come here, at no time had I faced any real reminder of home: none of the politics, snobbery or prejudice that walked with me on my day's existence in London had followed me here thus far, and I suddenly felt that this evening might remind me of just that.

Kato and myself were the last to arrive, but at least we were not late, our appearance almost dead on time. As we entered the back of the house, through the large kitchen, the place was awash with people, cooks and serving girls racing back and forth in preparation for the evening's festivities.

Mary noticed us and waved to us to come to her. She was stood next to a well-presented woman, dressed in what looked like expensive looking blue and green African robes and a green, silk headdress.

"This is Julius' wife," Mary told us.

Kato and myself greeted her politely.

"Thank you for helping tonight," she said in return. "I know my husband values your assistance. I will let you get ready. The guests should start to arrive in around an hour or so. Mary here will pass on to you what I have told her. If there are any problems then let her know and she will find me."

We all nodded as she then politely made her excuses and departed, our hostess calmly walking around the kitchen tasting food and making last minute checks on the preparations, whilst talking quickly in Swahili.

"How many people are they expecting?" I asked, leaning forward so as not to make too much noise.

"Around fifty I think," Mary replied.

"That is quite a few," Kato said. "I had no idea the boss knew so many important people."

"You will probably know most of them as they come to the bar," Mary continued. "There should only be a few who you will not have seen before. Maybe the ones who live out here nearer the beach."

I nodded.

"We should take a look around, just so we know where everything is."

Kato agreed, so as Mary led the way, we left the noise and chaos of the kitchen behind us.

The first of the guests did indeed arrive an hour later, pulling up in large cars: their drivers depositing them at the gate before pulling away to park further along the road.

As the evening progressed, I got into my job for the evening, trying to forget my earlier anxiety as I served drinks and snacks to African, European and Indian. I felt quite anonymous as I moved about the crowded room, and occasionally watched as Julius and his partner worked the room like the good, professional hosts they were: talking to everyone, introducing themselves, smiling constantly, making sure their guests were well fed and watered.

I was a silent partner in a dance that took in the diversity of three continents, presented in a kaleidoscope of colours: in styles of dress, types of foods, and ways of manners and being. I was a witness to all of this and found myself catching snippets of Hindi, Swahili and Italian, whilst noticing rich silks talking to casual linens and expensive cottons. Curries with Indian spices were served, whilst chocolate cakes emerged that has an almost French flair for design.

Julius and his wife had spared no expense in attempting to make this as grand an affair as they could to impress their guests, and I was an eager witness to it all.

The fact I was hidden also gave me the opportunity to eavesdrop on conversations, listening in as local dignitaries discussed the politics of the day, information that gave me a more rounded view of the world I was now living in.

"Like that new woman, the Albino lady they've hired," said a heavy set man who was sweating profusely, even in the air-conditioned room. "I'm not sure just what her role is to be. Why is she in the government? And who is going to pay for her?"

"She is there to show those fools up north that they cannot keep on murdering Albinos to get rich," answered a lighter skinned man, who was perhaps Indian, though I couldn't really tell. "All these stories about Witch Doctors cutting off Albino arms and legs to make their magic, it's a disgrace, and it's making us look a laughing stock. I even hear the BBC ran an article on it for one of their channels."

"I agree, they are making us look like idiots," added a woman, possibly the 'Indian' man's wife. "They always show Africa as either poor or backward. There is so little respect for us."

"Well, I like the idea of the government taking a stand against these fools up there," interrupted the heavy set man, whilst obsessively dabbing a napkin at his forehead. I handed him another pair of tissues to assist him. "Thank you. The government should try to do more to re-educate these people up there near Lake Victoria though. I hope the woman they have taken on board realises this."

"It's not an issue of education," the countered the Indian man. "It's one of poverty. The Tanzanians in the north have no money, and they see us with so much more. The only way forward is to provide better means for them to support themselves. Then they won't rely as much on some of these stupid, outdated, superstitions."

I found myself drifting around the three of them as they continued their debate, recalling how narrow and superstitious a view I myself had held of this continent. Those movies and stories I was always told as a child about how backward Africa was: the ways we as children used to call each other 'African' as a means of putting each other down: the visions we had on television and in the news of African being poor or untamed and unfriendly.

As I handed the woman a drink, she continued. "I agree. The more money the government can plough into regions like that constructively, then the more chance they have of avoiding situations like this one that has arisen.

"It is good though that they are employing more women in the government now. It is a positive sign to send to other women and girls around the country. They need role models to help them realise what they can achieve. Look at what the Japanese are trying to do with their donation up in the Morogoro Region."

The fat man nodded furiously. "Yes, wonderful gesture of goodwill. Their Ambassador was hopefully right when he said that building a hostel with that money would reduce the hardship for female students and encourage them to concentrate on their studies.

"Hopefully it will keep them away from the boys as well. Too many of these girls run into dangers on their way to school. Rape and the possibility of contracting Aids, being forced into marriage because of unexpected pregnancies: we shouldn't be exposing our people to these dangers in this day and age. It just isn't right."

I took my leave from the three of them at that point, my job done, my stay overstayed, as I thought I might be in danger of having my prying ears discovered. As I moved through the party, I caught the eye of Mary, who smiled at me warmly, whilst serving an excited looking young boy with some finger food as his mother knelt down next to him and whispered something in his ear.

I thought about her, considering what she had told me about her own life here in Tanzania, and wondered for the first time just what types of dangers she had faced as a young girl. I knew from our many intimate talks that her world when growing up was very different to mine. She walked nearly 10 kilometres to go to school in Kitwe as a child, normally with a friend but also occasionally on her own: whereas my mother accompanied me on the journey of less than a mile to mine. She travelled along worn tracks in the morning heat, whilst I braved only the daily traffic and occasional rain or snowstorms.

We had very different lives, Mary and I, came from backgrounds as diverse as I might imagine, yet here we were, in this city, in this room, at this time, the pair of us, a couple, dating, seeing each other, making efforts to meet each other.

I smiled at her as I thought about this, impressed by my newfound courage, by my belief in myself, and my willingness to trust this woman.

She looked up at me right then, noticing the look on my face, and studied me. Our eyes meeting for just a few seconds, before the boy tapped her on the shoulder, asking for some more food, dragging her attention away from me.

It was all I needed from her. That attention was enough.

"It's a success!"

It was nearing midnight, and Julius was with us in the kitchen, rubbing his hands excitedly as he paced up and down, and clapping people on the back as he passed them. The evening over, he had discarded his jacket, his shirt open to reveal a hairy chest alight with little droplets of sweat.

His wife, who was stood nearby, clasped her hands together as Julius walked over to her and embraced her warmly.

"It was a success, wasn't it my love?"

"Yes Julius," she replied. "Everyone there seemed to have a good time tonight."

Pleased with the response, Julius kissed his wife once more. "Then you have done well tonight my love," he continued, before turning to the rest of us. "All of you have. Take tomorrow off work and help yourself to whatever is left over."

Kato, who was standing opposite me, leaning on the overworked, but now cool, stove, clapped his hands to show his pleasure before rushing inside to grab all that he could carry. "Karl, do you want to give me a hand?" he shouted.

"I will be there in a second," I replied, extremely tired.

"Just leave us a few things for tomorrow!" Julius' wife called out around the door.

Together, Kato, and myself picked up a few left over bottles of wine and one of champagne, whereas Mary had found a plastic bag from somewhere and stuffed it with as much food as she could carry.

"Where are you going with all that?" Kato asked.

"My neighbour is ill," she replied. "I told her about tonight and said I would bring any food left over just so she had something to eat tomorrow."

"That's good of you," I added.

Kato didn't seem so sure as Mary walked past him and returned to the kitchen, the bag in her hand.

"Something is wrong with her," he mused. "She doesn't seem herself at the moment."

"What do you mean?" I asked.

"Well, have you noticed anything funny at work recently?"

"No," I replied honestly. "Everything seems the same as usual. Why do you ask?"

"Because money has started going missing from tills."

I stared at him incredulously. "What? And you think Mary is involved?"

"Keep your voice down!" Kato said sharply. "I'm not saying anything. All I know is something is wrong and Mary hasn't been herself, not since she has been with you."

"Well, she has been fine with me," I countered, in just as sharp a manner. "And I'm not sure I like what you're implying."

"I'm not trying to offend you, my friend. It's just that there is something going on at the Miami. Even Julius has noticed it. Just be careful, that is all I ask."

I found myself glaring at him. "Let's go home," I replied firmly.

Together, the three of us caught one of the last buses back to the suburban city area of Dar Es Salaam. The bus was almost empty, except for a drunk and sleeping couple who looked like they had been out to the beaches to the north for the day and were on their way home.

The driver was a short man, quite young, and wearing a Chelsea FC shirt. I smiled at his back as it reminded me of my one visit to The Shed when I was a teenager.

Also on the bus was a skinny looking Tout, all buck teeth and wild hair, who had come across as more than a little annoying when he had first stopped to pick us up. At the next bend in the road the bus came to a halt once more, and an elderly man boarded, shuffling along the row of seats until he found a place just in front of us.

The Tout, who from the look of his eyes, may have even been drinking, then started berating him in Swahili, hassling him for his fare, which the man swiftly paid him. But that didn't stop the Tout, who continued to gesticulate and point at him.

"What is he doing?" I whispered to Kato, who was seated behind me.

"He is drunk and a bit of a bully," my friend replied softly in my ear. "There has been a lot of that lately, with the Touts harassing anyone they feel like for almost no reason at all. Sometimes the only reason they stop is because the passenger has given them a little more money to do so."

"That's illegal isn't it?"

"Yes, but the police don't want to know about it. They often turn a blind eye to these things."

"I think it is so unfair," Mary added. "They even did it to me once a few months ago. I had to give them double the fare just to make them stop."

"What do they do if you don't pay them?"

"Then they bully you some more, and eventually throw you off the bus."

Suddenly, the old man cried out as the Tout struck him, his arm raised and ready for another blow.

"Don't!" I cried out, standing up in my seat.

"Karl!" I heard Kato whisper sharply.

Mary's hand grabbed at my leg at the same time.

The toothy Tout turned towards me and said something in Swahili whilst swaying slightly.

"Don't do that again," I continued.

"You only speak English," the Tout sneered. "Where are you from? America? We hate Americans here!"

"Don't hit that man."

The Tout glared at me. "You can't tell me what to do!" he shouted walking menacingly towards us.

"What is going on back there?" shouted the driver.

The Tout said nothing, instead giving me a toothy glare.

I glimpsed back over his shoulder to see the elderly man preparing to get off. As the bus came to a stop, he glanced behind himself nervously, then quickly alighted.

The toothy Tout poked me in the chest with his index finger. "Now you owe me double for that lost fare American," he said, imitating my supposed New Yorker accent.

"Don't do that," I told him firmly.

"Do what?" he continued, this time poking me twice more.

I hit him with as firm a blow as I could have mustered in the confines of that bus, sending the Tout staggering backwards.

As he fell he reached out for something, grabbing at the seat the old man had just vacated, his momentum forcing him sideways and downwards, before he struck the ground with a thud.

As the driver rose from his seat, I raised a hand, stopping him in his tracks.

"Don't," I said calmly, before turning to my companions. "It's probably our stop anyway."

Mary and Kato looked at me, their eyes wide open, and nodded, following me as I calmly walked along the bus, not even considering the dazed toothy Tout whose feet I had to step over.

When we were on the road once again and the bus had departed Kato started laughing.

"What's so funny?" I asked.

"I have always wanted to do that," he replied.

"So have I," Mary added. "I'm just glad we didn't get hurt in the process, sometimes they are armed on these buses. What made you stand up to him like that?"

"I don't know. It just felt like the right thing to do, as if that is what you do."

Kato was still laughing. "Well, I now know who to call if I am in trouble. You can do that for me anytime."

I looked down at Mary. Whereas Kato was almost apoplectic with amusement at what he had just seen, she was more reserved, scared even. As we walked home, I tried to grasp her hand in an attempt to reassure her, but she didn't respond.

She didn't pull away from me, but she didn't respond either.

Interlude

Email
From: Your Mother
Sent: 7th September 2008
To: Karl T

It's been over two months since you left and I still haven't heard anything from you. I feel as if you have deserted me in my time of need, as if you are ashamed of me, or something. When I went to the Magistrates Court last month I was told the wrong time so arrived three hours too early. I asked the people there what was going on and was told the case wasn't to begin until 2pm, not at 10am in the morning as I had been informed. On my own, I decided to go home and wait, then went back later that day, to be met by a lady from Victim Support and the man from the police. I gave them both a piece of my mind for not telling me the right time, and even though they apologised I was really very angry with them. The policeman told me what was supposed to happen: I was due to stand up in the dock and tell the magistrate or judge what had happened, before your father would do the same. He also said I could have gone home as I didn't need to be there beyond giving my testimony. Then we were told that the case was being adjourned as your father's solicitors had only just received their papers and had not had time to go through them thoroughly. The case was therefore put back till 30th of September.

Busta came to see me the other day, which was good of him. He did a bit of shopping for me, and asked if I had everything that I needed. I told him I was doing well and didn't want to bother him too much. You are lucky to have a friend like him, as he is such a good boy.

The only other person I've told about everything that has been going on is your Aunt Ruthie, and she suggested that maybe your father is starting to lose his mind. I've been trying to cope as best as I can, but need you here to help me. There are bills starting to pile up, and the Water Board have been on the phone regularly asking about outstanding debts from a couple of years ago that your father never paid. All of this just goes to show how useless he has always been. For all these years I've lived with him, he has never taken me anywhere or given me anything: all the things I have I've had to buy for myself. Now, I find out the full extent of everything. The house is falling apart: for example, the windows need doing, the garden needs a good tidy up, and the front of the house needs a painting. These are all things he said he was going to take care of years ago, but never did. I often wonder why I married him.

The bad dreams have also started again. Each time I have one it seems to be worse than the one before, and for the last couple of nights I've been too scared to actually go to bed and have begun locking all the doors and sleeping with the lights on. I wish you were here to help me, as I feel I need your support now more than ever. It's just too difficult to go through all of this alone.

I hope you are well wherever you are now.

Mum x

Email
From: autonews@willesdenherald.co.uk
Sent: 24th September 2008
To: Karl T

Exclusive interview with Nelson 'Nelly' Jackson, son of Brent MP accused of numerous gang crimes in the borough, by Neil Pullman.

My interview today is with Nelson 'Nelly' Jackson, the teenage son of our own MP for Brent. After his conviction for the shooting of Mr Bennie Davies, aged 17, a crime that was reported in the Herald on the 23rd of July, Nelson 'Nelly' Jackson, stated that he wanted to talk to the press, and in particular myself as he had read a number of my articles in the Herald.

At first I was reluctant to take on the story. Visiting prisons is never the most pleasant of experiences, and I really had no idea of why Nelson wanted talk to anyone at all. He had done the crime, been caught and convicted for it, and was now going to spend at least the next several years in prison. On further investigation though, I discovered a more interesting angle. Nelson Jackson felt he wanted to use the forum presented in order to talk about his family background as a fatherless boy from the Black community, a topic that has been commented on by everyone from the leader of the Conservative Party to Barack Obama. He wanted to give his side on why he had turned out the way he had, to present an additional 'perspective' on why he committed the crime he was convicted of.

"I hate my father," was the first thing Nelson said to me after we sat down.

We were in a plain room with plain, brown padded walls. There were no pictures, and no windows, just a table and a couple of chairs. A prison officer stood impassively nearby, watching over us as we talked.

I recalled right then why I hated prisons so much. It was their oppressiveness, the ugly plainness of it all.

Nelson looked just as he should have done: like a boy barely beyond his teenage years, his head shaved, his eyes bloodshot, his skin pockmarked with hormonal spots. I almost felt sorry for this waste of a life, but I didn't.

"Why do you say that?" I asked him in reply.

"Well, he stands up and talks about just how important it is to be good parents, how vital it is to get knives and guns off our streets. My father will stand there alongside all those other hypocrites, those MPs and white people from Parliament and just lap up the limelight. I think he enjoys telling other people how to run their lives, but he never did anything for my mother, my brother and me, he never did anything for his own family."

"Didn't he ever support you all?"

"No," Nelson replied with a solid shrug. "My mother struggled. She worked really hard without him. He only rarely gave her any money for things like clothes and food. She had to work two nursing jobs in order to put food on the table and keep clothes on our backs."

"Is that part of the reason you fell into crime?"

"Partly. I think it was something else though. My father used to beat my mother when I was a child."

When he told me that, I knew my hunch was right, that I was onto something interesting. "Do you mean regularly, or just as a one off?"

"It happened quite a lot of the time when my brother and I were kids. He would come home from work some nights, and wouldn't say a word to us as we ate dinner together. He would just sit there silently, looking down at his plate and pushing his food around. Then when us kids had gone to bed we would hear them: they would argue at first, then the fighting would start, there would be crashes and things would be smashed. They were both at it though, we always heard both their voices: from my mother's cries to my father's anger. My brother and I were so scared we sometimes used to climb into bed together to comfort each other. On other occasions when I was alone I used to wet myself I was so frightened."

I was surprised by the level of candour coming from this still young man as I sat there and listened to him, but still I wanted more. "Did your father ever used to beat you?"

"Yes," he replied, hesitating momentarily. "They both did. Our father, when he was still around, and our mother when he had left and we were starting to grow up a bit, maybe when we were around 10 or 11. Dad barely spoke to us, but often when we were playing up he would come in and shout at us, call us disrespectful, and beat us. It was to teach us to defer to him, he would say. I was glad when he finally left."

"Why? He was your father after all."

"Because it was too confusing. Yes he was my father, but I didn't care for him, and he didn't care for me. He always kept his distance from us. He only engaged with us to beat us. All I wanted from him was someone I could relate to, someone I could spend time with on a Saturday afternoon playing football in the park. All I got though was someone I was afraid of, who if I even sneezed wrong would beat me for it."

"And your mother?"

"Well, she used to take her anger out on us when he wasn't around. Tell us we were worthless, that she wished she had not had us, and that she could have been so much more if she didn't have children. Then, after he left, she found the church and was out of the house even more than before, leaving me to look after my brother. Oh, she would cook for us and leave food in the house, but she was always away from the home. She used to run a service for the homeless of Harlesden, helping them to pick themselves up with the assistance of God. Meanwhile, my brother and I were out on the streets, playing with friends, then getting into mischief, then falling in with the wrong crowd."

"What do you think of her now, your mother?"

Nelson sneers at me for the first time during our interview. "She's a hypocrite man," he replies. "She is out there saving the whole fucking world, and yet all she did for us was to leave us in the cold. She was as bad as he was really. I saw her sitting in the gallery at my trial, all tears and hugging her friends, but she wasn't there for me. She wasn't there for me then, and isn't there for me now. She was there for herself. To make herself look good, to stop herself feeling guilt for leaving us like she did, for beating and abandoning us like she did."

We fall into silence, so I leave him there for long enough that his words sink in, before I catch the Officer glancing at his watch, telling me my time is almost up. "Tell me about this 'wrong crowd'."

"Well, they're my boys. I respect them, they respect me. I know that I can rely on them in a time of need, or at least I thought I could back then."

"You mean, they're not here for you now?"

"No, they're not. I haven't seen any of them since I was caught. But back then we were tight man. We ran together, and we looked out for each other. It was like living in a family. They were my brothers and sisters, my fathers and mothers. We looked out for each other."

"So is that what led you into a life of crime? Is that what made you shoot Bennie Davies?"

"No. You have to understand, if I was scared of my father, if I hated him that much, then I would probably be scared of most other men, I would probably hate them too. When that kid…"

"Bennie Davies…"

"Whatever. When he crossed my path we started arguing, and I wasn't going to let some punk kid on a train try to get one over me in front of my boys. These were the only people I respected, not that kid. He started it. He started acting like a big man and wanting to embarrass me in front of my boys, and I wasn't ever going to let someone humiliate me like that again. Not after my father. Not after my mother. So I took him down. I shot him to show him who was the man there. I let him know who was in charge."

"And do you regret it?"

Nelly laughed at that question. It was a strange sound, a slightly mad sound, like the Joker or some other mad megalomaniac in a bad B Movie. "Hell no. I don't regret it. He was a chump. He got himself shot. He should have been big enough to take me on, but he wasn't. I got to him first, so I'm still here. I still have both my legs and I'm still standing tall. I'm still a man."

And at that appropriate moment, the Officer in the corner rises, and I realise that my time with Nelson 'Nelly' Jackson is up. I conclude the interview, shake his hand, and leave him there in that horrible place. My anxieties no less confirmed by that prison, or by that boy who inhabits it.

Fifteen

His name was Andreas Horst.

I discovered this when I saw them together that time. The pair of them, naked in bed, lying side by side, her leg draped over his as she lay on her back, his hand over her breast as he lay on his stomach. They were sleeping when I entered. Sleeping as a baby cried in the corner of the room.

With that room bathed in darkness, with only whispers of light sneaking through the makeshift curtain, I walked over to the cot. The child looked up at me, noticing me, but didn't stop crying. I stared down at her hoping, but my new pain, this deep ache, didn't end. We regarded each other, and I imagined us seeking solace in each other, before any bond is broken, and her tears again ran free.

Mary was strange with me for a while after I last saw her.

It was week after the incident on the bus. Kato had told everyone about it, making me a bit of a celebrity in the Miami, as the customers wanted to know in glorious details just what I had done.

"Good!" said Julius when he heard the story, shaking his fist as if it was his own triumph. "Those Touts have been bullying passengers for a while now, and they should have been stopped a while ago. My wife was even assaulted by one recently. If I had been there I would have done the same as you."

"Well, I hear the Police arrested some people yesterday," Kato added. "They said there had been too many complaints and they've had to take action."

"Is that right?" I asked.

"Yes, look," said one of the newer regulars as he handed me a Guardian newspaper.

"Thanks." As I read the article on the inside I found even I was surprised by what I had done. Standing up to those men as they bullied someone weaker for money riled me, and I needed to do something about it. I wanted to help, almost needed to in fact, the drive to do so being so strong yet so subtle at the same time. It was as if I was almost born to do so.

Yet, as we discussed my good deed, as the crowd of men and women in that bar debated the lack of manners creeping into Tanzanian society and I listened, I noticed that one person was absent.

Mary was there in the bar, but she just kept on working. I glanced over to her, hoping to catch her eye, but she just kept on moving between the other tables. She maintained her station, serving the other occasional local patrons, and those one time travellers that often came by.

She never looked up at me. Never looked over to see what I was doing, to catch my eye in return, hold it for a second, before looking away coyly. None of the things she used to do were there today, and that left me feeling a little nervous.

We had not been together since that night of Julius' party, and I realised just how much I'd missed her. Mary had told me she was going away to visit her mother for a few days, so she wasn't at work, and even though I was occupied at Miami, whatever free time I did have I spent on my own.

We tried hard to be discreet about our relationship, although most of the team there knew, and I think even Julius suspected something was going on. Kato would only occasionally ask me how things were progressing, allowing me space and telling me what I did in my own time was my business, which I respected of him, so I knew I could go somewhere with my problem.

"Sometimes she is very secretive, Karl, you must have realised this by now?" he said to me when I asked him about it during a lull in business.

"No," I replied. "I hadn't. You've known her longer than I have you know."

"Yes, but I've never gotten as close to her as you. Yes we get on well, and in some ways she is like a younger sister to me, especially as we've worked together for a good long time, but it is rare for her to talk to me about anything."

"Has she ever?"

"Only a couple of times," Kato replied with a shrug.

"Can I ask what about?"

"I think it was about money. She wanted me to lend her some to send back to her mother as her family were having a problem."

"And did you?"

"Of course. And she paid me back soon afterwards, so there was never any problem."

"I wonder if that's why she is so quiet now?" I mused. "I wonder if she needs my help in some way, but is struggling to ask me?"

"You should find out. She is your girlfriend after all."

As that day progressed, I found I wanted to surprise Mary, to come to her home after work and see her. I had missed her and felt the desire for us to reconnect with each other. The nights we had spent together had been important to me, helping me suppress some of my guilt about not being in contact with home, as well as bringing me further into my life out here in Dar Es Salaam.

Mary's shift ended in the late afternoon, and as it was early in the week many of the patrons present departed soon afterwards as they made an effort to be on time for work the following day.

As we were fairly quiet therefore, I left work a little early, excusing myself to Julius, before walking through the warm night to the Barclays Bank, one of the few in the city with a Cash point. Once there I found myself fingering my rarely used card, remembering more expensive days back home, before I pushed it into the slot, and drew out some money both for myself and to give to Mary.

Then I drifted back to the main road, and caught one of the buses heading out of the commercial district. This time, the Tout on the bus was well behaved. In fact he was almost overly polite to me, as if he had heard the news about his colleagues and decided to curb any enthusiasm he might have held towards assaulting his passengers.

After twenty minutes I arrived at Mary's stop, and disembarked, taking a walk through the grim poor neighbourhood she lived in. Dogs littered the street, and rubbish was strewn everywhere, whilst water dribbled along makeshift drains carved a long time ago into the dry earth. As the smell of the street began to assault my nose I found her place, remembering the first night I had walked her back here.

I could hear a baby crying for its mother, the sound almost painful to witness as if it were in real, life threatening, discomfort somewhere, yet even thought several lights were on nearby, I couldn't tell where the baby was.

Walking up to the shack she lived in, and with soft lights shining from inside, I knocked on the door. It moved under the light tap of my knuckle, the door swinging leisurely away from me.

"Mary," I whispered out, as soft as possible so as not to disturb any of her neighbours.

Receiving no answer, and fearing something was wrong I walked inside.

The lights were coming from several candles lit in her sitting room. As I walked in I noticed them, flickering in the occasional breeze that drifted in through the doorway, their life almost over as they neared the small holders they were situated on. Two glasses were sat on the table next to them, one finished, the other still half full, and the smell of alcohol permeated the room.

My heart began to race as I saw them there, those glasses, sitting next to each other, almost touching but not quite. Expensive glasses in an inexpensive setting.

The cry of the baby seemed to rise again, this time from somewhere closer.

My mouth dry, my hands beginning to sweat, I drifted on automatic out of the room and towards the bedroom. Hoping not to, and knowing I would hate what I would find I walked there, my slow deliberate steps almost painful. The baby seemed to beckon me, its pain drawing me in as if I were its mother. It was in this house, I now knew, in the other room.

Mary had a child.

"Why didn't she tell me?" I whispered.

As I entered, the bedroom was almost dark, with several shafts of light sliding through the old curtain far across the room. The bodies were there on the bed, one black one white, both naked, both sated, the smell of sex still heavy.

I walked over to the baby, naked and lying in her crib, still crying, still in so much pain, and looked down at her.

We watched each other, before I bent forward and picked her up, cradling her head as I lifted her towards me, her tears ceasing almost instantly as I did so. My thumb moved on its own, drifting over her face to wipe away the tears that so smeared her lovely face.

"Why didn't she tell me?" I whispered to the baby, wishing she could answer me.

"Who are you?"

I turned around suddenly.

The man on the bed had risen and turned on a light at the side of the bed. He was now sitting bolt upright, as if ready to pounce on me, but seeing that I had the baby in my arms he hesitated.

Mary stirred beside him. "What?"

"If you want money let me get it, then go. Don't hurt the baby!" the man continued, this time with more authority.

"I'm not here to hurt her," I replied.

Mary then awoke, grabbing at the sheets and pulling them over her to cover her nakedness. "Karl! What are you doing here?"

Turning around, I placed the baby back in the crib. "I came to see you," I replied. "I didn't know that you had a child Mary, or that you would have company."

Suddenly seeing the situation differently, Mary's demeanour changed, moving from one where she was indignant, to one where she was embarrassed.

"Who is this man?" said the chap on the bed, his accent stronger now.

"My name is Karl," I replied directly to him. "I'm from London. And you are?"

The man looked older in the light, his blonde hair short and messy, his face that of a man in his fifties, his paunch now hanging out on the bed. "I'm Mary's boyfriend, Andreas. I see her when I come to Dar Es Salaam."

My heart dropped. This was her boyfriend. This man, this white man, was seeing this woman, this African woman, this woman who I'd become attracted to, who I wanted to be with.

"Is this true?" I asked vainly.

Mary just looked at me sadly, before nodding her head.

Andreas regarded us both, first me then her, studying us as if noticing something. Then he rose from the bed and pulled on a pair of trousers hanging over a chair nearby.

"I think you two had better talk, don't you Mary?" he said firmly.

Mary just nodded again, whilst her baby gurgled in the crib behind me.

His eyes on me constantly, Andreas pulled on a shirt, grabbed his sandals and left us alone, still leaving the door open just in case.

We stood there in silence Mary and I, with my staring at her, and her avoiding my gaze, her nervousness and my rising anger in conflict, jousting for position. It felt as if I wanted to tear her head from her shoulders, but dare not to because she looked so delicate sat there on that bed.

"Why didn't you tell me?" I asked finally.

"I don't know," she replied softly. "I didn't want to hurt you."

"And you really think my seeing you in bed with another man doesn't hurt?"

"I'm sorry."

It wasn't enough. I was frustrated with her, angry at this woman I had come to like, had come to imagine something different with, a life with, a life where we could build something together, not just me rescuing her.

"Oh no."

Mary looked up at me. "What is it?"

As I rubbed my forehead I realised something. "I've done it again."

"What, Karl?"

"Nothing," I replied, nodding my head in the direction of the open doorway. "Who is he anyway? How long have you two been together?"

Mary shuffled nervously. "Over six months now. Andreas is German. He works here on business, and when he is in town I see him."

"Does he live here in Dar?"

"No, Nairobi. He is married. Has a son in Cologne as well."

My head shook as I chuckled to myself. "So, you're his mistress then?"

"Don't say it like that?" Mary countered, as if protecting her honour.

I wasn't having any of it. "Well, its true isn't it?"

"No, it's not. Andreas loves me, and I love him."

"If he loves you so much then why doesn't he leave his wife for you?"

"He will, in time," Mary replied. "For now, I just have to be content with seeing him when he is here."

I thought for a minute, pacing the room as I tried to understand the situation I had put myself into. As I walked around that room, I felt like an animal, its prey caught with its back to a tree. I could have struck at any time, raced over to her and devoured her, put her out of her misery even, but I didn't. With her other man in the room next door I chose not to. Yes, that was the reason I didn't murder Mary right there.

"What do you get from him?"

She looked at me shyly. "What do you mean?"

"What do you get from him?" I replied, with more sharpness than I intended. "What does he give you in return? He has a wife up there in Kenya, comes here on business, stays with you for free, eats your food, fucks you when he wants to, so what do you get in return?"

"He doesn't fuck me! He loves me!"

"Tell me," I replied, stalking closer towards her. "What does he give you in return? Is it money?"

"Karl…"

"Tell me!" I shouted, now not caring if her fucker of a boyfriend heard me.

Mary just looked at me though. With sad, moist eyes, she stared at me, with that sheet still pulled tight up to her neck. She looked like a frightened fawn caught in my angry red headlights, a creature that knew it was lost, that knew it was about to die. "He gives me money, Karl. He gives me money, because I need it to pay for the medicine for my child."

"Is that what you wanted me to do as well, to give you money? Is that why you spent so much time with me?"

"…………yes…………"

Stunned, I just stood there, hands by my side, my mouth open, floored by her honesty, destroyed by it actually.

I was right about myself. I was correct that I had found another woman to rescue, had smelt out someone who needed me, no, who needed my help, my money, my assistance to make their world better. It wasn't me they needed, it wasn't me they even wanted, the me I had used to attract them didn't exist in Mary's mind. It wasn't the me who so wanted to be a good partner, to build a new life, and to add this relationship to the jigsaw that was becoming his life. That me didn't exist in her eyes, in Mary's world: that me was invisible, except for the wallet, the wealth that a boy from Britain might have brought with him.

Remembering the money I had so readily collected from the Cash point earlier, I felt myself groan again inwardly. It was so predestined, so unconscious: I so readily went to her aid even when she didn't need me, and maybe even already knew about this child in its crib behind me.

I turned towards it and away from her, to the baby and against its hateful mother, staring down at the dark brown eyes that gazed up at me sleepily, and reached into my pocket. Fishing out the notes, I counted out one hundred thousand Tanzanian Shillings, and rolled them up tight, before tucking them into the crib beside the baby.

"She needs these more than I do," I said calmly. "Just make sure she gets her medicine."

Then without turning back, I left the room and walked next door.

The bastard named Andreas was sitting cross-legged on the sofa, drinking something left over from one of the two glasses I had seen earlier. He looked up at me steadily, his eyes holding an almost colonial hold over me, as if they radiated a distinct type of authority I already knew. "Have you finished?"

"Look after the child," I replied.

He stared at me coldly, with barely disguised contempt. "Just get out," he said to me finally.

I faced him there, almost willing myself to destroy this son of a bitch sitting here in this house with Mary and her child, but I couldn't. I couldn't destroy this network, this little mini organisation, designed as it was to save a child in a crib, to help one of the sick young born to a poor woman from Tanzania.

Another woman I couldn't save.

So, walking out into the lonely night, I left them to it.

Sixteen

It was the guilt that forced me to leave Dar Es Salaam.

The guilt that I wasn't enough to save Mary; that I wasn't able to be there for her and her child: that I didn't have enough for them; that she didn't trust me enough; or that she believed her Germany boyfriend better able than me to be there for them both.

That guilt, that pain that raided my throat, that choked me the following morning after I last saw Mary, and stayed with me during the next few days, until I decided to run away.

Until I decided to run away, again.

It was such an intense feeling that I had to take a couple of days off work. It had me bedridden, and even Kato was astonished by it, his questioning eyes worried about my sudden illness.

With the days passing slowly, I only rarely ventured out, choosing instead to stay indoors, to mull over my thoughts, to wallow in self-pity a little. Guilt, I still felt it daily. I still wished for something, something that would stop me from feeling this way, from crying in the darkness and the light. I still wished for something to take the pain away.

"Why couldn't it have been me to save her?"

I heard the words as I showered one morning a few days later. Standing there under that mere trickle of water I knew them, felt that phrase, sensed their presence, as if they had come from somewhere within me, somewhere younger, somewhere trapped and now set free.

Shaking my head to rid myself of more than just the soap, I pledged that it was time for me to get out of the house, and get some air. Locking myself away was beginning to get to me.

I took a bus into town, getting off just near the Askari Monument, and walked towards the Botanical Gardens, a rare green space in the Commercial District, and somewhere I had been maybe once before with Mary. Remembering this stunned me, so I diverted my path, instead entering a nearby Internet Café where I decided to check my emails, perhaps seeking out some correspondence from home to take my mind away from my present problems.

My plan was a failure. My mother had written to me.

Reading those words from home hurt me more than I realised. They amplified the anxiety and guilt I was already feeling about Mary.

Here I was thousands of miles away, and there my mother was as home, suffering, struggling through the most difficult time of her life. Endeavouring to force herself through a criminal trial against her husband, my father, and needing me by her side to protect her.

To be there for her, like I had always been.

To protect her.

Quickly moving on to the second email, the local news from home, changed nothing either. Ire was all I was left with after I read through the interview of another stupid Negro, another boy just like my father, and fathered by a man just as stupid as my father.

I paid for my half an hour before I was anywhere near finished and left, continuing my stroll to the Gardens, and turned left. Passing numerous palms and other sign-posted exotic fauna I sought out somewhere solitary to sit. Landing heavily on a dry, old wooden seat I just gazed out on the world, letting the distant noise of traffic drift away, and enveloping myself in horrible thoughts and emotions.

Guilt. That binding force, that deepest of horrible feelings. The one used to tie me to my mother so that I didn't leave her side, that I didn't leave her undefended, so that she wouldn't have to suffer the bad dreams she was now enduring.

My guilt should I fail to protect her from my father, this was the thing that kept me by her side for so long. A man in his mid-thirties tied to a mother who needed me.

Yet, what was it that kept me away?

I suddenly recalled that night, several nights before, when I was there in Mary's house and she humiliated me, when she let me know just what an artificial role she wanted me to play in her life. I recalled how even Andreas dismissed me. How he saw me as no threat to him at all, and how I let him think that. Suppressing the one emotion I felt for him, I let him dominate me with just a few words.

My anger.

It was fine for me to show it on the bus. That was an obvious case of bullying and needed to be dealt with: that Tout fucker deserved the headache I gave him. But didn't Mary deserve to see how angry I was as well: didn't she have a right to see just how much she had hurt me.

"That is how I got here," I heard myself say, and it made sense.

My anger. That is what kept me going out here, that is what meant I couldn't go home. My angry self rescued me, it helped me to get away, it gave me the chance to experience something new in my life, to be something more.

My anger versus my guilt, these two warriors fighting to the finish within me, vying for overall dominance within the world of Karl.

Yet I was also losing.

The guilt. On days like today I could feel it, its pull titanic, its depth unfathomable, its tie to me unbreakable. How could I ever be free of it: how could I rid myself of that need, that desire, that role I played so well for mother and Mary, that one of saviour.

"You do know it's not your job to save them."

I was stunned as I heard myself speak, the realisation hitting me like a thunderclap.

Is it a son's job to save its mother?

Is it a man's job to save a woman?

Is it a son's job to stand between abusive parents?

Or is it the only way he will ever survive?

The lessons, and all I've learnt about myself. The times when I've wanted to leave home but haven't felt able, or found any excuse not to do so. The number of women I've rejected or kept at a distance just so I could stay tied to home.

All to avoid the guilt, all whilst suppressing the anger, all whilst sacrificing myself lest I don't survive, all whilst not realising that years later I'm still here.

"But I don't understand, why are you leaving so suddenly?"

"Because I have to get away Kato," I replied. "I've been here too long as it is, and just need to continue my journey elsewhere."

I was busy packing the last of my things into my bag, into that same sack I'd used when I first travelled to Zambia, together with another suitcase full of clothes I had accumulated during my time in Dar Es Salaam. I had no plan for what I was going to do, all I knew was that post my two day's sabbatical from work I couldn't stay here any longer. The pull to Mary, to my mother, was too strong, and I had to break it. I had to get away from it, to escape that pre-ordained need to liberate an other, that programmed position I had always held between my two warring parents.

Behind me I could hear Kato pacing about my room impatiently. I chose not to turn to him, choosing not to be face him as I didn't want to see his pain: it was enough that I could feel his concern about me leaving.

"You must stay," he said to me, pleading yet again.

"I can't," I replied calmly.

"But why? You haven't told me why, or Julius, or any of us. Is it me? Have I done something wrong? We can spend more time together if you like, I don't need to see Elsie every night. If you stay we can go and play pool just like you wanted to."

I heard myself chuckle. "That is kind of you, but the problem isn't you."

Kato continued his pacing behind me. "This makes no sense Karl, you arrive almost out of nowhere and haven't told us that much about yourself, and now you are leaving in just the same way." I heard him pause, and could feel the hairs on the back of my neck rise. "Of course!" he exclaimed. "You are leaving because of Mary, am I right?"

I turned to him. "What do you know about that?"

"I overheard her discussing something with the cleaner a couple of days ago, and when I walked into the back room they both stopped talking and looked at each other nervously."

I turned around. "What were they saying?"

"I didn't hear all of it," he replied. "But she did say something about fighting with you and some other European man."

I chuckled to myself dryly. "That is only part of it. She has a sick child, a baby, and is using the European for money. She would have used me the same way if I had not of found out about them."

"Ah, then this starts to make sense. Elsie said something to me recently about her. She had heard a rumour about a baby, but Mary never told any of us. But none of this is any reason for you to leave is it?"

"It's not as simple as that. I've always been there for others. I've always rescued women, stood between them and another, often male. I've been doing it probably since before I was even born, but there is a cost to it, and that cost is the loss of who I actually am myself. I don't know who I am Kato, can you understand that?"

"No I can't," he replied. "How will you always moving on help you to find yourself? Sometimes, you just have to stay and work through problems like this one. Sometimes pushing through tough times like this are what is important."

I turned back around and closed my bag finally. "I can't do that," I replied. "If I was going to stay here then I would have to see Mary every day, and that would hurt me too much. I was starting to feel something for her Kato, in fact I could have loved her, but she ended up using me in just the same way I'm used to."

Kato walked over to me and placed his hand on my shoulder. "Karl, I know she hurt you, but she is worried about you, especially as you haven't been at work all week. We're all concerned for you. Don't leave like this, please."

"I can't stay, my friend. I just can't," I said to him, feeling his hand on my shoulder, and the tears building uneasily in my eyes. I didn't want to tell him about my fear of losing control of my anger, of my sadness, and of destroying Mary with both of them. I didn't tell him about my guilt, my shame at not being there for her.

I didn't tell him because I was confused about them, just as much as I was confused about myself.

"Will we see you again?" Julius said to me sadly. "You were one of the best workers I've ever had in my bar. I will miss you."

"Thanks," I replied. "I will come back, I'm sure of it. This time though it will not be to work. This time I will let you buy me drinks all night."

Julius laughed, his round frame shaking. "I will look forward to that. Just make sure it is soon."

"I will."

Then he hugged me, a show of emotion that took me by surprise, and left me feeling a sudden regret at my decision to move away. Prising myself free of any transitory indecision, I disentangled myself from his grip, taking his hand and shaking it warmly.

This was the right thing to do, I was convinced.

It was an hour later, during the mid-afternoon sunshine, and I was preparing to place my bags in the back of the taxi I had hailed. Julius and his wife had come to see me leave, along with Kato, who was sitting on a nearby wall looking crestfallen.

I walked over to him as he jumped down.

"It's time for me to go now," I said sadly.

"I know," Kato replied, suddenly embracing me in an embarrassingly tight hug. "Look after yourself."

"I will."

Once I was free, I waved to the three of them and climbed into the back of the cab.

"Where are you going?" the driver asked me.

"The port," I answered, not totally convinced by my answer.

My lack of conviction probably translated through to the cab driver as he hesitated, looked in his mirror at me, and then shrugged. Then, finally, we pulled away.

As I waved farewell once more to my friends, I again felt that pain of loss, that sense that I was leaving, of sadness, and of just a little bit of excitement too.

For some reason, my thoughts drifted to 'Nelly' Jackson, shifting over to a boy in prison who I didn't know, but whose story in some ways mirrored mine.

Except for one difference, a major one.

I can feel.

I could feel the guilt and shame. I had been forced to sit and cry my way through that rejection by someone I wanted to be in love with. I could hold the guilt of not being there for a mother and father who in their own ways needed me. I was more than just an automaton, reacting to a stimulus in the only way I knew how. I was more than a boy who had decided that the only emotion I would be able to show was one connected to aggression.

I found myself feeling sorry for Nelson Jackson. Feeling sorry for his lack of feeling about himself or others, for the lack of guilt and shame that meant he felt it would be fine to pick up a gun and shoot that boy. That given his background, given his waste of space parents, he had bottled up all of his feelings, all that sense of loss, of shame, of guilt, of anger, and only allowed himself the expression of one of them.

Not to his mother, nor to his father, but to someone younger and defenceless, someone who he needed a weapon to defeat, a 17 year old student, weighing less than him, on his own whereas he had his whole ‘crew’, without a weapon as he had a gun. That bravest of brave boys, that weakest of pathetic men, sent out into a world ill-equipped and afraid of it by parents who failed to prepare him properly.

I felt for that boy, for Nelson. I felt his anger and his frustration. I felt for his future lives in and out of prison. I felt for the stigma that would now surround him whenever he walked the streets of the rest of the world. I felt the distance that some women would keep him at whenever he met them, and the disgust at the enthusiasm from those who would crave his crooked attentions. I felt the wary eyes that he would attract to himself whenever he walked into a shop or bar, and the idolising gaze that would alight on him from his peers. I also felt his rejection of these as they are not who he wants to be, and his frustration that he couldn’t make himself any other way.

And as the taxi pulled up at the port, and I disembarked, letting the driver remove my bags, before I paid him and tipped him, I felt his need to avoid that sense of loss that drove him to this extreme. It was that same sense of loss that had brought me here as well.

Here I was, on the busy docks of a major city, overlooking the dark blue sea beyond. I was just as lost as ‘Nelly’ Jackson, and just as frightened to find myself just as lost as he was.

Yet, as I grasped my bags and meandered through the crowds to the ticket booths, I knew that I understood myself far better than he did, that I felt myself a lot more than many other of my peers. I was more than them in that I would never hurt anyone else, and had no desire to. I was more than them because the route they were following was too narrow, too one dimensional, too limiting and clichéd: it wasn't for me, I didn't want it, and had never allowed anyone else to force me along it.

I wasn't scared of those feelings, in fact they excited me, they kept me moving forward to look for myself more.

These feelings.

These feelings

These feelings that set a grateful Negro free.

PART THREE

Email
From: Your Mother
Sent: 20th October 2008
To: Karl T

Well, I suppose you may have heard by now that the Magistrates Court found your father guilty of abusing me. What you may not have known is that because he has a clean criminal record they did a series of tests on him and have discovered that he is suffering from Dementia. The doctors say that his illness may be the reason why your father is so angry right now, and why he spends so much time talking about the things he thinks I have done to him in the past. They were worried about signing him over to myself, given both our ages, but they have prescribed him a course of medication that they say will work to reduce the aggressive impulses.

As for your father, I don't really think he wants to acknowledge how old he is getting, or that he has any type of illness. He is still a proud old man, so much so that he also still denies that he did anything wrong, and is as mean spirited as always. I do though think that his time in court woke him up a little, as he won't talk about it, and takes his medication regularly.

I am well. My scars have almost gone, though I suspect they will never fully leave me, and I have been receiving counselling though Victim Support. The lady there, a nice woman who is too young to be in that type of work if you ask me, gave me a leaflet on Domestic Violence, and even recommended a couple of websites to look at on the internet. When I read them, I never realised the lengths that abusive men go to, and just how much women put up with, it's been a total shock to me.

Karl, I'm worried about you. How are you? Where are you? Why haven't you been in contact with me? Even though I have taken over the house, and all the bills are now settled, I miss you being there for me. You were my rock. You were the person I could rely on most of all. In many ways you were like the husband I always wanted.

Come home soon please!

Your mother x

Email
From: Sally Riedler
Sent: 1st November 2008
To: Karl T

Hi Karl

I don't know if you will get this email, but I feel I have to send it anyway. I'm leaving London at the end of the month as I've been offered a job back in Stockholm, and after a lot of thinking I decided to take a leap and accept it. The money is less than here, the prospects are not as good, but it's closer to my family, and will hopefully take me in the direction I want to head personally. I'm happy to be going, but will be sad to leave London. I've had a great time here, met lots of good people (including yourself), and will miss the vibrancy of life in such a wonderfully diverse city, even if it is very expensive at times.

Why am I leaving so suddenly, you may ask. Well, my sister is getting married to a Danish man, something that has really made me take a good look at my life right now. I have to admit it, I'm jealous of her. She is my younger sister, for fuck sake. She shouldn't be getting married before me. Enya has never travelled, and only worked in Stockholm, but she is planning on doing something that I always expected I would do first between us. Herself and her fiancée, named Torsten, have already bought a place together, and are planning to start a family as soon they can after the wedding. He has a good job and can support her, and she really wants to be a mother. All of the things I want, but have maybe never allowed myself. I've dated so many different men, and had some really good times, but never once considered the possibility of having a relationship like theirs, and I have to say that it hurts. So I want to go now and give myself a chance.

I know that no one has heard from you since you left (not even Busta, which I am surprised about), and hope nothing bad has happened to you. Karl, out of all the men I've met here, you will be the one I will miss most of all (we had some great times didn't we?). Wherever you are I do wish you well for the future. Write to me if you get the chance, and if you ever make it to Stockholm then look me up.

Take care
S x

Email
From: autonews@willesdenherald.co.uk
Sent: 30th November 2008
To: Karl T

Brent MP Resigns!
Charles Jackson, the MP for Brent, resigned in a flurry of publicity last weekend following further revelations about his private life. Mr Jackson was at the forefront of the initiative in Brent to try and reduce violent crime in the borough; being the driving force behind empowering the police to search schoolchildren, increased Stop and Search targets, and creating a detailed initiative designed to encourage parents to take a close look at the role they play in their children's upbringing.

After months of speculation and numerous salacious stories about Mr Jackson's personal affairs, the Brent MP resigned his post following meetings within his own political party. Mr Jackson made a statement last night saying, 'Following the press hounding of myself, and my family, it is with great regret that I have decided to leave my post after two years. I would like to thank all of my constituents and colleagues for their support during my tenure as an MP, but feel that now is the time for me to look for other avenues of work.'

Beginning with the story of his son, Nelson 'Nelly' Jackson, who was accused and convicted of the shooting of Bennie Davies earlier this year, and Jackson Jr's subsequent interview (which was first summarised in this paper), additional tales about Mr Jackson began to emerge. These included interviews from his then partner, some of his ex-girlfriends, and even a number of his other children, outlining his negative attitudes towards them all, and especially, it seems, towards his offspring.

A spokesman for the XXXXXX Party said in a statement released on Monday that: 'We feel that following all of the adverse publicity Mr Jackson has received, and in the wake of the work he had put in to make Brent a safer place for its populace, that in order not to appear hypocritical he should step down from his position forthwith. We would like to thank him for his endeavours and wish him all the best for the future.'

Mr Charles Jackson was born in Oxfordshire as the son of a Civil Servant. Educated abroad, he then moved on to Cambridge where he studied law, before becoming a barrister in the borough of Brent for several years. Mr Jackson has informed the Willesden Herald that he intends to return to law and that he has not fully turned his back on the idea of becoming an MP in the future.

Seventeen

"Mrs Taylor, I'm so sorry for your loss. You know I cared for Karl, but I can't believe that he's done this to you, not after all these years. You're his mother after all. He should respect you. You brought him into this world. For him to just run away like that is so wrong."

"Thank you Lilly. I just want my son back now. I miss him so much. I hope you understand just how much."

"I do, oh of course I do. He was my boyfriend after all, and I really did care for him. Yes we argued sometimes, and yes we occasionally didn't speak to each other for days on end, but I did care for him. Sometimes though I felt he didn't respect me enough, and that did bother me. Perhaps that was the reason for us never settling down together."

"So you miss him?"

"Yes, occasionally I do. Though I struggle to admit it, I have to say, and he could make me so angry sometimes. He was just like my father; stubborn, ignorant, and really argumentative; and he was also like my ex-partner too. My son is growing up to be just like that. I don't know what I'm going to do with him if that boy starts getting into trouble. I've thought of sending him to live with his father, but I know he won't look after him like I do.

"How are you coping without Karl?"

"Not badly. I've always managed to get by financially, even without the money my ex owes me. Karl would normally give me some extra, especially when he stayed with Reggie and myself. Now that both of them have gone AWOL I just have to tighten my belt a bit, but I will get by. I always do. My job is as secure as any job would be in the public sector, and if I really need any help then I'm sure I can get some at my church."

"What do you mean?"

"Oh, you wouldn't have known. I've joined a local Methodist Church. Nice congregation, good sermons, and the Pastor's very helpful. It's something I've wanted to do for quite a while. When my friend took me a couple of months ago it felt as if I had come home. Mrs Tucker, finding God has been the best thing to happen to me. I go as often as I can, maybe three or four times a week now. I just love it. Maybe you should come with me sometime."

"Thank you dear, maybe I will one day, but what about Reggie?"

"What about him?"

"Well, who looks after him when you're at church?"

"Oh, he can take care of himself. There is food in the fridge for when he comes home from school. Then he has his homework to do. I'm sure he copes well enough without me.

"Aren't you afraid he will just end up on the street with the other local boys?"

"No. I'm sure he will behave. If he doesn't he will have myself and God to answer to."

"Hmmm, quite. When you rang me, you said you had heard something about Karl's job?"

"Oh yes, I almost forgot about that. It was only a rumour, but I heard that Karl had resigned his post at the Charity a couple of weeks ago, via email. Sent it to the Director, who then told one or two members of his team the news. Seems they were expecting it as he had not been in touch for a while."

"Do you know what the email said?"

"No, not at all. Sounds like it was brief, just covering his desire to leave, his thanks for the time he's spent there and sending his best wishes to us all for the future."

"It seems strange that he didn't send you anything? Especially considering you were dating for a while."

"I know, I have thought about that. Maybe he just didn't know what to say to me, or maybe he wanted to say goodbye to me separately. I don't know. Perhaps I will receive something from him soon."

"Hmmm, I'm sure you will."

"Marco isn't it? Thank you for seeing me. I'm sorry for all the emails and calls, it's just that…

"Listen, Mrs Taylor, I don't want to sit here with you, and you don't want to sit here with me, so let's be clear about something. It's my wife that's made me talk to you, so why don't we cut out the crap and get on with this, so that we can both get back on with our lives, alright?"

"Oh. Yes. Alright then."

"You wanted to ask me about your son?"

"Yes."

"Well, let me tell you from the start, I thought your son was a fucking idiot. "

"Pardon?"

"He was an idiot Mrs Taylor. I knew that from the moment I first saw him, when he got on the fucking bus with us back in Lusaka. I knew then that he was going to be trouble on our trip. Whoever heard of a black man coming on a trip to Africa with a load of white people anyway? I'm surprised they allowed it."

"Marco, I think my son just wanted to go away by himself for a while. What can be wrong with that?"

"Lots! Know your place I say. My father used to tell us that about your lot, and I agreed with him. If he'd had his way, we would never have sent that bloody Windrush back to the West Indies to collect you all. Once you had done your bit for the Empire, once your boys had died to keep Britain away from the Nazi threat, then we should have packed you all back off to your little islands and left you there. You didn't deserve to live in a civilised land like ours then, and you bloody well don't now."

"What do you mean?"

"Well look at you all. Your boys are the ones out on the streets with guns and knives, shooting and killing each other. All those teenage girls who seem to end up in the papers because they became pregnant before they could even qualify for a GCSE: all black aren't they? The highest rate of Schizophrenia and drug abuse is from within the black community. And I even read somewhere that the highest rate for suicide is for young black men. The mark of an uncivilised people that is: you people really don't know how to be around others."

"What does this have to do with my son?"

"Everything! He is part of you, and you are part of the problem. I even remember when I was a teenager my father was based near Lincoln and for a short time we used to live just outside the town centre. There used to be a gang of us that would chase your lot through the streets if we saw them, especially if we thought they were trying to get off with one of our girls. God help them if we caught them. Then we definitely made sure they got a kicking."

"Listen, Mr…"

"All I'm saying Mrs Taylor is I think your son is best off wherever he is. He insulted my wife and me when we were away on holiday, something I will never forgive him for, the bad mannered little shit. If you had taught him better he probably wouldn't have run away from home like that, I mean really, a man of his age. Who does he think he is, Robinson Crusoe? Leave him wherever he is I say, forget about him. He isn't worth the skin he's inhabiting."

"He's my son…"

"So what? I have a son too, and have done exactly the same with him, especially after he married that Hindu tart. What right has he to call me old fashioned?"

"I'm surprised. You mean your son married someone who isn't white?"

"What? Oh, yes, he did. Some girl from India. Never met her though. When he told me, I threw him out of the house. Told him he could only come back when he left her."

"How long ago was that?"

"………..two years and three months……….and twelve days now………..''

"I'm surprised that you chose to travel all this way Mrs Taylor."

"Well, I'm just glad that you had the time to see me Kerry, especially at such short notice. You said something about moving on from Johannesburg soon."

"Yes, well I intend to move up to Nairobi in the next couple of weeks. I've been offered a teaching post at the University there and have decided to take it."

"Have you been a teacher for long?"

"Not really. I used to hold a post lecturing in Kampala for a number of years, but then I gave it up to get married and returned back here to South Africa."

"Well, I hope the job goes well for you. When do you start?"

"Thank you. I begin in January. They want me to come up as soon as I can after the Christmas holidays so I can meet the rest of my department. That will also give me some time to orientate myself and settle in. In many ways, it was your son that helped me decide to take this position."

"Really?"

"Sure. Mrs Taylor, I really felt for Karl when I met him. He was a good man, but still a boy in many respects. When I looked at him, I mean when I really studied him, he didn't have the feel of a man, he didn't have a man's build, or a man's presence. He came across to me as much more immature than that. What he did have though was a sense that he was looking for something."

"What do you mean?"

"Well, I remember one day when we were travelling to Victoria Falls and the bus broke down. We had to wait two hours for a replacement to arrive, so in the meanwhile a few of us, including Karl, decided to visit a nearby local Orphanage. I recall whilst we were there the look on your son's face whilst he sat there with one of the children on his lap. I don't remember how old the boy was, but Karl seemed to put him so at ease that the child just played with him as if they were father and son. And when I looked at your son, I saw for the first and only time on our trip, just how relaxed he could be when he allowed himself. He was in his element there, at ease with himself, and yet as soon as we walked back to the waiting buses, that side of him was gone."

"...................I'm touched by your kind words for him."

"He is a good man, your son, but he is searching for something. I think he is looking for himself, and maybe just needs to be out here on his own. That is why I wanted to meet with you Mrs Taylor, to tell you that I don't think you should worry about your son, and that I'm convinced he is fine without you. Go home, let him be, I'm sure he will return home in his own time."

"How do you know that? He could be out here on his own and really need me for all we know."

"Because I saw it in his eyes. I talked to him about this when we were in Lusaka. I talked to him about taking a chance to find himself, about asking himself a few hard questions. Your son seemed so unnaturally scared to me Mrs Taylor: scared of living, scared of growing up, scared of being whoever he was meant to be.

Your son had so much potential within him that he didn't seem to be using, and being on a trip like ours wasn't helping him. He was living in the same bubble the rest of us were. Yet he didn't need to be there. Karl is a capable man. He just needs some time to find himself, that's all."

"Well, I hope you took your own advice Kerry. It seems yours may have cost me my only child."

"Oh, don't blame me for Karl leaving you Mrs Taylor, he made up his mind about that one all on his own. He is a grown man after all."

"He is just a boy. He is my boy. He will always be my boy..........."

"............then that is why you have to let him be."

"Maybe. Did he really inspire you as well?"

"Yes Mrs Taylor. I'm not a hypocrite, I could never do that to myself. Hearing those words in my head prompted me to leave my husband Randal and take the job in Kenya."

"Thank you for taking the time to meet with me. What is your name again?"

"It's Kato, Auntie."

"Auntie? I'm not your auntie, so please don't call me that!"

"Sorry, I don't mean any offence. This is just the way we relate to our elders here in Tanzania, Auntie. Any man or woman who is older than ourselves, yet is not of our family, we call Auntie or Uncle out of respect."

"Oh. Right. I didn't know that."

"That is alright Auntie."

"Hmmm, I'm still not sure I like it."

"Maybe you will get used to it."

"Maybe."

"My boss Julius told me that you wanted to talk to me about something."

"Yes, I understand that my son Karl worked here for a while."

"Karl? Oh yes, he worked with us for six or seven weeks, not very long. We used to live together as well."

"Really?"

"Yes, Karl was a good man. I really liked him. It was sad to see him leave. We all talk about him here at the Miami. The patrons, they always ask when 'English' is coming back (because that is what we called him). They all want to know if any of us have heard from him. Even Julius mourns him a little I think."

"Why?"

"Because Karl was an unusual man. He stood out from the others here. We could talk about many things with your son: like politics, and music, but we would always talk about football. Did you know your son is an Arsenal fan, Auntie?"

"………..no, no I didn't know that."

"Well, your son would always try to tell us that this year was going to be their year. Myself, I am a Manchester United fan, but we have many Chelsea and Liverpool fans here as well, so we would always talk about this with him. He would tell us what was going on back in England, and even explained to us just why the England Football Team had not qualified for the European Championships (Karl was very depressed about that, he told me). It was good for us to have him around, and even the takings went up when he was with us."

"I'm glad my son was such a good worker, especially in a bar like this."

"This is a good job Auntie. Not many people are able to find work here, never mind in a bar, so your son did very well. You should be proud of him."

"Quite…"

"Auntie, you must try to understand, not many black men come from Britain to Tanzania, and nobody understands why. In fact, the last time I met any black people from your country Auntie was two or maybe three years ago, and even then I almost didn't realise she was British."

"What happened?"

"Well, I was with some friends at a club one time with my girlfriend and a new friend of hers whom she said was from out of town. As the night progressed, this friend seemed to become more and more moody, as if she didn't really know what she was doing there, so I asked her what was wrong. We started talking, and I had no idea that she wasn't from Africa, her accent wasn't any different to mine when I spoke to her in English, although I did think it was a little strange that she didn't speak Swahili."

"How did you find out she was from Britain then?"

"Well, she told me. At first I was really shocked. Here was this beautiful African woman standing with me, talking to me like she was from Africa. Sure she was wearing European style clothes, but lots of people do that here, so it is not that unusual."

"Did she mind that you didn't realise where she was from?"

"Auntie, that is the strangest part. She hated that I had not said she was from England. She said that it left her feeling as if she was anonymous, as if she suddenly didn't have an identity. She really didn't like the fact that she was able to blend in for the first time."

"Hmmm, interesting. And do you think Karl was able to hide himself here?"

"No. Karl was a different person really. I think he enjoyed being able to talk to people here, but I don't think he totally wanted to fit in. He was far too proud of who he was to want that, and especially of his football team!"

"Well, if he was so happy here, what do you think happened? Why do you think he left so suddenly?"

"Karl never told us why, Auntie. All I know is that Mary took a lot of time off work soon afterwards."

"Mary?"

"The woman he was seeing whilst he was here."

"Oh, I see."

"Auntie. I think he was in love with her, and I think she broke his heart, so that is why he left."

"What did you do to my son?"

"Auntie, I didn't do anything to Karl, you have to understand, I really did care for him."

"Then Mary, why don't you tell me why you drove him away?"

"I didn't mean to! I was desperate!"

"Desperate for what?"

"Money!"

"What? So you used my son for the money he could give you? What were you going to use the money for? To buy clothes? To make yourself look better than the other Tanzanian tramps out here? Why don't you tell me why?"

"No, auntie, it was nothing like that. I needed the money for a special reason."

"And what reason was that? Why don't you tell me Mary? Afraid I might find out the truth?"

"…………………"

"Nothing to say now? Too ashamed of what you've done?"

"………………..I did it because my daughter was ill. I needed the money to pay for her medication. Because she had malaria."

"You used my Karl because you have a sick daughter? Why should I believe you?"

"Because it's true! I wouldn't lie about this. Ask anyone. Ask my neighbours, they know the truth!"

"Then where is he Mary? I must find him. Where is my son?"

"I don't know. I wish I could tell you, but I don't know."

"…………………"

"I miss your son Mrs Taylor."

"What? After what you did to him? How can you say that?"

"Because he was good to me. Because he looked after me. Your son wasn't like the other men I've dated. He didn't just use me for sex and leave me like my ex did. He didn't disrespect me when we were together. He was a good to me. He had respect for me, led the way for me. He was so very un-African and I found that attractive in a man."

"Then what happened?"

"I don't know. I wasn't used to being treated so well. I met Karl at the wrong time. I'm so ashamed of myself. I feel as if I can't tell you any more."

"Go on."

"I had given up on finding a good man, and once I'd given birth none of the men around wanted me anyway. So I used myself. I gave myself to men for money, using them as they used me, especially the European ones. I used to meet them in the bars up the coast, and always made myself available to them. They would sometimes give me money, or sometimes make sure I was looked after in other ways. Andreas was one of the men I liked most of all, and in the end he was the one I settled with."

"And you used the money to pay for the medication."

"Yes. For my child. You have to believe me."

"………………."

"When Andreas found out about Karl, when they met the last night that I saw your son, he left me as well. Both of them ran out of my life. The only two men in the world that have ever cared for me: one financially, one with my heart. I hurt them both, and they both left me."

"Where do you think Karl went?"

"I'm not sure. I heard a rumour he may have travelled south."

"A rumour? From whom?"

"From someone at the docks. We used to go there sometimes and just watch the water. He liked that, watching the waves crashing against the shore, said he found them meditative. I have some friends there and they used to see us together. I can give you their details if you like?"

"Please. That would be very helpful."

"I have them right here. Let me write them down."

"……………………"

"……………………"

"Thank you. I will contact them as soon as possible."

"My pleasure. Auntie, before you leave, can I ask that you do one thing for me?"

"Depends on what it is."

"I know you may not want to do this, but if you find him, can you tell Karl that I'm sorry. I really didn't mean to hurt him."

"When I find him I will do so."

"Thank you."

"My pleasure. Mary, one last thing, what happened to your child? I see no sign of her here."

"……….. she died six weeks ago Auntie. She did not survive the malaria."

Eighteen

"You have to keep using the bucket, otherwise we will sink!"

Mudi's call woke me from my daydreaming, shifted me away from smelling change drifting in on the breeze: a change in the weather or a change in my fortunes, I didn't know which. It was mid-afternoon, and the sun was high in the sky, beating down on the pair of us, its force tanning my dark skin darker. I grabbed the 'bucket' from behind me in the dhow, which was only called a bucket because it was made from plastic, had a makeshift plastic handle and looked vaguely like one. Then, I recommenced my job of scooping out the water and throwing it over the side. That repeated endeavour, though mind-numbingly boring, kept me amused in a strange way: a regular effort to ensure that we didn't sink: or a replicated gesture to certify that we would make it home with our catch for the day.

My friend, the elderly Mudi, sat opposite me, pulling the dark triangular sail tight to catch the wind, his head shaking with amusement and bemusement at me, his first mate, his colleague. His gestures replaying his pride and mystification that a strange foreigner who looked like him could ever want to sit in a boat like this and do a job like his.

We had been out since morning, Mudi and I, awoken by the sound of 'my' dog Hobo as he shuffled about outside our home. And as we lay there with the dawn approaching, we could both hear Hobo's paws scratching at himself furiously, could hear him walking around, and could imagine him circling himself a couple of times before he once again lay down to sleep.

Mudi was the first to rise, as usual, his elderly nakedness soon covered by what I would call a sarong, but which suited him in a more masculine way than I could have imagined. As always, he would then walk outside, secretly patting Hobo on his way, before going down to the coast in the weakest of light to wash and do his ablutions. Then he would bring back some fruit for our breakfast.

Whilst he was gone, I would like there in bed, listening in to the morning chorus, before rising and putting on some tea for us both to drink before work. Then I would join him on the beach, shit, sort of shower, and maybe have a shave, as the dawn sunlight rose on the south coast of Tanzania.

Then we would begin our work for the day.

I had been staying in a set of beach huts on the coast for a couple of weeks when I originally met Mudi.

Treating myself to a holiday within what had already begun as one, I had withdrawn yet more of my money back in Dar Es Salaam and taken myself away, catching yet another bus from the station: heading in yet another unknown direction with a pocketful of cash, and a large bag full of clothes.

It felt good to be leaving Dar: my experiences there having taught me so much about life in Africa, and about myself. Although I was sad to no longer be at the Miami, I had made some good friends there, met some interesting people, and enjoyed the conversations we always had: those debates we would undertake between shifts, be they about football, politics, or just the state of things in Tanzania. They would talk, and I would listen, or I would talk and they would listen, and we would exchange views, share jokes, tease each other and generally enjoy each other's company.

The problems started when I fell in love with Mary. I should have known there was something wrong. From the beginning, when I first met her, she was always secretive and distant. Looking back on it now, maybe it was only because I had no one to rescue that I felt drawn to her, that my mother wasn't around, so I needed someone else to save, and she fitted the role like a shoe to a foot.

Yet there was room around this boot. It didn't fit right, and it never would, hence maybe why Mary felt the need to have another man in her world: a man who would pay for her, who would support her and give her money to buy medication for her sick, yet beautiful, child.

When I left I hated her, but as those two weeks passed I began to feel sorry for her, to feel sorrow for some of the women in Tanzania, and in the world at large, that they would need to prostitute themselves in such a manner. I felt pity, a pathetic pity, for a pitifully poor breed, my more cynical, nasty side coming through, aiding me in my separating from her fully.

It was then I decided to take a trip out to one of the islands off the coast, so I asked several of the locals, using my still very bad Swahili, if they knew of anyone who might be able to take me, for a fee of course.

The one name that kept coming up was that of Mudi, so armed with directions I went to find him, locating him in a small village not far from where I was staying.

"You are the foreign black man everyone has been talking about," he said in good English on seeing me for the first time.

When I met him he was sewing up some of the holes in his fishing nets, sitting on a rock outside of his home: a building nothing more than a shack, built from coral, barely finished, and with a roof made from a mixture of corrugated iron and branches. He was an old man, maybe in his late fifties, thin yet still muscularly built, with the body and visage of a man who had worked outside all of his life. When he smiled he showed a set of clean white teeth which bellied the rest of him though.

"My name is Karl, but yes, I guess that would be me. I see you speak good English."

His concentration seemed to return to the net at his feet. "I know it yes, though I don't use it that often. My name by the way is Mudi."

"Nice to meet you," I said offering him a hand which he didn't acknowledge. "Well, I'm looking for someone to take me out to some of the islands for the day. Can you help?"

"How much are you paying?"

"Twenty thousand shillings," I replied, knowing full well I would have to negotiate with this man further, as everyone else had done on my trip: from the stall holders in the local village where they sold fruit and vegetables, to the tout walking along the beach who wanted to sell me soap and then a porn CD Rom.

"Done."

"What? Shouldn't you be bartering me upwards by now?"

"No need. I know a good deal when I see one," he replied. Then the man placed his net on the ground, before rising from his stone and walking inside his home. "I will pick you up at daybreak tomorrow. Please be ready."

And with that, our negotiations were over.

The next day, as we sailed out from the shore, through the clear turquoise sea and out over the reef in his old wooden Dhow, Mudi took the time to tell me a little about himself.

"I'm not from here. I was born and educated in Dar. I only settled here after university."

"Why?" I asked him, strangely puzzled by his admission that he preferred to stay here in this desolate place than strike out for something more.

"Why not?" he replied, smirking at me. "My father wanted me to become an Engineer. Yet after spending three years studying I decided I didn't want to do what my father wanted me to, so I returned to my village and decided to work alongside him. Besides, Dar is a smelly city. It is too busy and there are no decent jobs. Even if I had decided to stay it would have been a struggle for me to do well."

"Well, it is busy, I will agree with that. But you should see London sometime. Now there is a place that is busy, smelly and can be quite crazy."

Mudi laughed, his teeth on show again as he pulled the sail tight. "I can imagine. You must tell me about it as we travel."

"And you must tell me about your life here."

So that is what we did.

We swapped stories about London and Tanzania, more of the tales like the ones I had heard in the Miami. Mudi told me the local gossip: about one of the women who had not born her husband a child and what a scandal that was: and I told him about the only scandals I could remember from when I last checked: the latest edition of Big Brother and the ever present news on the Beckhams.

As we sailed out towards a set of white beaches crowned with small bunches of palm trees, we got to know each other, and I came to enjoy the company of this simple, yet educated, man.

The day moved on, and Mudi showed me beautiful island after beautiful island, taking me out to some of the reefs so I could snorkel, catch a fish (my first, a small pitiful crab that had lost a claw and wasn't moving that fast in the first place), and just relax. I was having a glorious day, the first day in a while that I had managed to forget my troubles.

My blissful reverie didn't last long.

"What brings you out here, my friend?" Mudi asked, as he loaded the small Dhow and we prepared to go home.

"Out where? I'm just on holiday," I replied, calmly sidestepping the real reason.

Mudi though was having none of it and shook his head slowly. "No, that is not the truth, and you know it. Very few people holiday on their own like you do, and especially not men from England like yourself," he said, shaking his head. "No, you have a story to tell. There is a reason you are here."

As I loaded the last of the bags back into the boat and we pushed ourselves away from the last of the islands, I thought about what he was asking.

I had been through so much on this journey. I had dipped a fearful foot into waters that drew me into this voyage of self-discovery, like a child who swam in choppy waters and became trapped by the unseen undercurrents: those pulls beneath being the tougher times: the days when I was able to drift and watch the world go by being the better.

Now, I'd worked myself free to some degree, and broken the surface, hiding out here in the south of a country I was beginning to respect, coveting parts of myself that I was starting to discover.

I felt free here. I felt liberated, unburdened by that cultural responsibility placed on such narrow shoulders from the days before I was born. I felt cheerful, and able to walk the ground without fear of cutting my feet lest a blood relation beat me for making too much noise, for having a cold, for just being there: lest an abusive guardian in an abusive relationship take their abusive anger out on myself.

I no longer cared about home. I didn't miss it, I didn't miss them, and I was no longer surprised by this deepest of realisations. So when Mudi's question came I felt momentarily confused and unsure if I wanted to answer him.

"Are you sure you want to hear such a story?" I replied, testing my new friend, seeing if he really had the shoulders to hold what I would be about to tell him.

Those thin shoulders of his though just shrugged nonchalantly. "Of course. I would not have asked otherwise."

So I told him it all. I told him about mother, about father, about the abuse that happened and my running away from it. I told him about my past, about my present, about my time in Dar Es Salaam and my love for another woman who used me. I told him about my sadness, about my pain, about the loss of myself that had happened along the way and my efforts to rediscover some part of it.

I told him as much as I thought he could handle from me, then I told him a little bit more.

"You must come and work with me," he stated casually when I had finished.

"What?"

"Is your hearing going from all that noise in London? I said you must stay with me for a while. Come and work with me. I could use some assistance and you look like you need some help too. We could work together."

I was quite shocked by his suggestion. "I'm not a fisherman," I stammered in reply.

But Mudi just laughed. "Neither am I Karl," he said smiling. "Neither am I."

Hobo turned up two weeks after I left my shack on the beach and moved my few things over to Mudi's home in the nearby village.

As we returned from a day of fishing, I stopped on the beach to catch my breath and adjust my catch on my back, taking in the ladies still harvesting the seaweed in the harbour. As I watched them I recalled just how poor they were, and how wretched their lives often could be.

One of the locals waved to me, a woman in a colourful green dress whose name I could never remember, but who was with us the night we danced around the bonfire when Obama was elected.

As I returned her greeting I smiled at the recollection, noting how even out here, even on the coast of Africa, the news of a black man, a black African, becoming the most powerful man in the world was great news indeed.

For one night, the hotels relaxed their ban on locals coming inside, so I partied, drank, and danced with Canadians, Americans,

Africans and Europeans, all together as one, all happy that the Bush years were over; that a new era had begun.

But weeks later, here she was that same woman, planting lines of sticks planted in the shallow surf before the reef to gather crabs, seaweed and anything else they could sell at rock bottom prices to the local hotels. Like us, like Mudi and I, they were now back to living from hand to mouth, making barely a living whilst the greedy hotels all along the coast went back to making huge profits out of their work.

"Get away from here!"

Turning around, I saw Mudi him kicking out a foot at a dog that seemed to be doing nothing more than play-biting him. The little brown and black dog of indiscriminate type that seemed to just run about him as Mudi directed an irritable foot at him from time to time.

I couldn't help but laugh.

"Don't encourage him," Mudi said irritably.

"He is nothing more than a puppy," I replied.

"Humph! He is probably just as scruffy and flea bitten as the rest of his kind around here."

I looked down at the dog. Now it had decided to jump up at Mudi and see if he could make him drop any of his fish. "Well he seems to like you." Then putting my catch down, I took out one of the crabs and broke its shell before scooping out the meaty innards with my hands.

The dog ran over to me excitedly.

"Here you go boy," I said, before placing the meat out on a piece of shell for him to eat. "Don't finish it too fast, there's no more to be had after that lot."

As I stood and gathered the rest of our catch, I noticed Mudi looking at me and shaking his head.

"What?" I asked him, pleading a type of innocence.

But my friend just looked at me incredulously, before correcting the load he was carrying, and walking on up the beach ahead of me.

The dog was outside our home every morning after that. It would stand guard all night, sometimes only pretending to sleep I suspected, and would bark angrily if anyone came too close that he didn't know. Each morning, in a lame attempt to reward him, I would feed him something to tide him over until Mudi and myself returned from our day fishing out to sea.

"He is your dog, so you have to look after him," Mudi had told me once he had relented on my numerous requests to keep him. "No one else here has seen him before, so he is a free dog. But I will not be taking care of him."

"That's fine by me," I had replied, feeling more than just a little bit of excitement, feeling as if I was a teenager all over again.

"But tell me, why the name Hobo?"

"Because it suits him," I answered, not wishing to divulge the truth: that Hobo reminded me of 'The Littlest Hobo', a strange American children's television show about a dog that travelled alone and had adventures. As I thought about the name, I wondered just how much it reminded me of myself, and my own journey. I often smiled at the realisation.

The three of us lived together like a little family, Mudi, Hobo and myself. We enjoyed each other's company, but worked very hard, with Mudi taking our daily catch out to the village to sell if it was only small, or if it was larger he would head to one of the nearby hotel chains.

The money we made often wasn't very much, but Mudi was pleased with it.

"With this we can buy some Sweet Potatoes and some rice," he would say for example after a particularly good day. Then, whilst I went for a run, taking Hobo with me, he would prepare a stew of some kind using whatever fish we had left.

Often, we would build a fire on the beach, and just sit there underneath a blanket of stars talking, alone the pair of us, two men chatting about stuff, about ourselves, about our histories and our possible futures.

"I will probably die here," Mudi said one night. "And that is fine for me. All I ever wanted was to remain, and I am happy here. My life has been good enough."

As I ate that night's offering, feeding Hobo who was rolling around besides me, I turned to him. "What would have made your life better?" I asked him.

"Only one thing."

"What?"

"If my wife had survived."

It was the first time Mudi had ever mentioned a partner of some sort, and that surprised me. As we sat before the fire I saw this man visibly shrink before my eyes. This thin sinewy black man with more strength and energy than I could often muster, suddenly looked old before my eyes, and that left me feeling shocked.

"What happened to her?" I asked him tentatively.

"She fell ill and we had to take her to hospital some years ago. She was only supposed to be there for a routine operation, to remove her Appendix if I remember rightly. When she came out though I knew instantly that she wasn't the same."

"I don't understand."

"We had been together for many years Karl. I met her when I was at University in Dar. She was beautiful back then, all dark shy eyes, and feminine. I loved her from the moment we first met. We courted during that time, and then married soon after we both graduated, deciding not long after that we didn't like the city. I brought her here to this place, to my home, and my parents were so proud to have us here. It was a happy time. Even though we had no children, and even though we wanted them, we were still happy, and I always loved her.

"Yet, when she fell ill she was different. When the woman I loved returned from that horrible dirty hospital carrying the AIDS I knew she was changed forever, I could feel it."

I sat back slowly, unable to hide my shock. "I don't know what to say."

"I had spent all of my money on making sure she was well enough from the operation, all of our savings for a rainy day like that one. So there was nothing left when she fell ill, there was no money for me to buy her any medicine to help her. I tried going back to work in the city back then, tried to find a way, but no one would hire me. Engineering had moved on since my qualification, they said. I couldn't even get a job selling newspapers on the streets.

"I felt so ashamed that I couldn't help her, so I didn't return home for quite a while. I just hid there in the city for weeks, months, not contacting her, not sending any money back. She was on her own. The woman I loved was on her own and I didn't want to be there as she died."

We sat there in silence that night, with even Hobo catching the mood, taking himself off for a while, as I just watched Mudi. I sat and stared at this brave, yet sad old man before me. The latest person to befriend me, to take me into his home and treat me with such kindness.

"How long has she been gone now?" I asked finally.

"Over ten years I think."

"You never remarried?"

"No," Mudi replied. "I could never do that to her memory."

"Hurry there, do you want us to sink?" Mudi repeated sharply, but still with a hint of humour in his voice.

These revelations from each other, me about my past and my parents, Mudi about his and his wife, helped bring us closer together. So as I sat there in that boat, bailing out water from its leaky bottom I didn't care about the monotonousness of it all, I didn't care about being bored fishing out at sea each day.

All that mattered was that I had moved on from those dark times dealing with my parents, from being their referee, to being Mary's saviour. I had found a place where I could hide away and belong, where life was simple and people were genuine.

Right then was the happiest time of my life.

Nineteen

Often after a day out fishing we would have to pass one of the checkpoints as we ported our catch to the nearest of the hotels in the area.

Approaching one, whilst on bicycles laden with produce, the man in his smart white suit waved to us to stop, directing us to the side of the road.

Obediently, Mudi did as directed and I followed him.

"You know what to do," he whispered over his shoulder, giving me the hint that I should let him do the talking until my Swahili was more competent.

The policeman, a heavily built man with thinning and greying hair who I had seen a couple of times before, approached us, his face a mask of concentration as always.

"Hijambo Baas!" was the last thing I understood, as Mudi and the policeman began their dance, a type of Swahili samba, with the pair bartering and negotiating.

Mudi held his arms open, palms raised in a gesture that suggested to me he was declaring that he had no money, whilst the policeman was pointing to the well wrapped up fish we were both carrying.

Occasionally, the policeman would tilt his head in my direction, and obviously say something about me that I wouldn't understand. Mudi would then smile politely, put a hand on my shoulder, and talk about me, probably excusing me from their discussion.

On this occasion though, the policeman was pretty insistent, so Mudi fished out a Thousand Shilling note from somewhere, before pressing it into the policeman's palm. Then his adversary in white waved us both by, and went about his business, promptly stopping a Suzuki Jeep that had just appeared on the road, its driver looking pensive to say the least.

"Why did you give him any money this time?" I asked Mudi as we rode away up the hill.

"Because I didn't do so the last time I saw him, and he remembered," he replied. "He even asked for some fish, but I didn't want to share any with him, so he told me he would have us both arrested if I did not give him anything."

"Sounds serious."

"Well, I think it has been a slow morning for him. He wasn't as friendly today as he normally is."

"What did he say about me?"

"He just asked who you are, so I told him you're a tourist who is staying with me for a short while."

Mudi's answer seemed strange to me as I had been living with him for a couple of months now. "Why did you say that?"

"For two reasons," he replied. "One, they do not like to harass tourists too much: it gives them and the country a bad name. And Two, because I know you will be moving on sometime in the future."

"How do you know that?"

"Because you do not belong here," he said softly.

With the surprise of his answer ringing in my ears, I let my bike fall back a little, so I could think. Something was wrong, I could feel it, and Mudi had not been himself over the past couple of days. He appeared anxious, as if he could sense something coming or changing, something negative. He was even being nicer to Hobo, which initially surprised both myself and the dog, although our four-legged friend in the end didn't seem to mind the extra attention.

As we rode, I glanced back over my shoulder, noting that the policeman was still there in his white suit, waiting for someone else to backhander. Mudi had said in the past that the police would stop us, would regularly try see if we had any money for a bribe, something that I had now learnt was common to this part of Africa. It was an occurrence that I came more into contact with the deeper I delved into this land. From the first hints whilst I was on my original trip with Kerry, Marco and the others, to the woman who was taken off the bus when I was travelling across from Lusaka, there was always a suspicion of something underhand going on.

Yet it was only when I came to stay with Mudi that I realised the fuller extent of it all.

"You have to negotiate with them," he told me when I asked about it.

"But why do they even ask?" I replied, a little naively. "Why not refuse them? Or just report them to someone?"

Inevitably, Mudi just laughed at me. "To whom? Everyone is on the take in some way or another, it is common knowledge out here."

"Is it?"

"Of course. Even the President is corrupt. They always want to remain in power, so they cosy up with whoever can keep them there, be it the police or the army. And then there are the businesses beneath him. They all come to him looking for favours to maintain their monopolies so they can dictate the price we all pay for goods, like food and petrol for example."

"And what about the police?"

"Well they are never paid enough, so they always look to make a little more from us. But you have to negotiate with them. If you were to pay them all the time then none of us would ever have any money, so it becomes a game. Sometimes you pay, sometimes you don't, sometimes you have to be forceful with them, and sometimes you have to give in."

"Hmmm, I really don't like it," I said pensively, feeling more than a little bit protective about my friend.

Mudi smiled as he put a palm on my shoulder. "It is the way Karl, a fact of life. And believe me it is worse in some areas than it is here. My cousin in Zanzibar told me that during Ramadan all the police are out on the streets collecting, as they have to give money at the end of the Holy Month. So the only way to get around this is to take more from the rest of us. It is a challenging time for him, and he is only a fisherman like myself."

I sighed at the futility of it all as we finally rode our bikes up to the entrance gates for one of the nearby hotels.

Mudi shook hands with the guard on the gate, before speaking to him swiftly in Swahili. After a couple of minutes, the guard then lifted the barrier, and waved us through.

"I will go and talk to my friends in the kitchen, see how much they want this week."

"Good, you speak the language. I wonder if they have a computer here."

"Ask at the reception," Mudi suggested. "They should have the internet there. Are you going to see if you have any messages from home."

I hesitated before I answered. "I suppose I should, although I'm more interested in how the Arsenal are doing."

Mudi laughed at me and patted me on the shoulder. "Well, check on Chelsea as well. I am sure we are beating you."

"Unlikely," I replied, before we parted company.

At the reception, the young lady behind the desk looked me up and down suspiciously, perhaps trying to work out what a scruffy looking local was doing anywhere other than the kitchens or the beach. When I talked to her in English, and explained what I wanted, she then seemed to relax a little, before taking some money from me as payment for half an hour on the internet in her office. As she left, she glanced over her shoulder at me, still not totally convinced by who I said I was or what I was doing there.

Taking some pleasure in her discomfort I then checked my Hotmail account, noticing the numerous emails that had landed in my Inbox since I last opened it some months before. Taking some time to delete all the Junk Mail, I then waded through to the ones of some importance to me.

It took an additional half an hour to look through all the proper emails, and it was just as Mudi came to collect me that I finished reading through them, including ascertaining that the Arsenal were top of the league from the BBC Website.

Mudi then told me he had sold nearly all of the fish, so in order not to lose any of our profits we decided to cycle back to the village via the beach, at least until we passed the checkpoint, before then heading back onto the road.

With the tide starting to move out again, I watched as the second wave of small ships departs the beach to fish well into the evening, marvelling at the beautiful sight of so many dark Dhows, their white triangular shaped sails resplendent.

The contrast strangely reminded me of Sally and her departing Email.

"She will be back home now," I whispered to myself, perhaps musing somewhat.

Right then, I surprising realised that I didn't care about her that much, and that I didn't miss her, mainly because I didn't know her really. She was someone I used to fuck regularly when I was going through difficult times with Lilly, or when I wanted my relationship with Lilly to contain a more sexual side, something she was always nervous of.

Sally was a good time girl, who wanted to live her life the same way many Western women did, fast and furious, with lots of money, lots of socialising, lots of trendy clothes and things to do: yet also with little feeling. And I too found that exciting, that freedom, that debauchery, that sense that I could do whatever I wanted, that I could be whoever I pleased.

Being with Lilly though meant that I often had to act a certain way, a way that didn't suit me, that I often found myself rebelling against, that often upset and angered me. Being with Sally gave me another option: I could be like everyone else, I could fit in, I could do the things, go to the places I wanted to, I could pretend to be the black bohemian prince I so wanted to be from my imagination.

Yet in the same way I didn't know Lilly, I didn't know Sally either.

That email she sent me was the longest one she had ever written to me, I realised. It contained more of a sense of who she was than she had ever let me see in person, and I learnt more about her wishes and desires in that page and a half of text than I ever had in a year and a half of fucking her.

Now, as she went home, as she left me behind, not knowing where I was, not knowing if I was safe or not, she felt secure enough that she could write these things to me. Now, she had ventured outside of her comfort zone and displayed her more vulnerable side.

And as we left the beach, and I rode that bike along the road, I found that I despised her for that pitiful attempt at intimacy, loathed her loaded use of language at a point where she knew there could be nothing more.

I imagined her not telling any of her closer friends any of these same things. I imagined her never uttering a single of those printed words to her parents, or, god forbid, her sister. I imagined her being the type of woman who would never say what she truly felt to any man, lest, she feared, that he use it against her: lest, she sensed, he might take that vulnerability and use it to bind her to him.

But most of all, in the same way that I realised how much I hated such shallow independence in a person, I suddenly saw, and because it was me who chose her, just how much it resided within myself.

Feeling a sudden need to be alone, I excused myself from making dinner and went for a walk, with a quizzical Hobo following along behind me.

The sun had almost set, so I gathered some sticks and dug a hole in the sand of the beach, before building a small fire to keep me warm.

Sitting there under the emergent starlight, listening to the distant waves wash against this shore, I couldn't help but let the email from the Herald drift into my thoughts.

I had read about the Charles Jackson with interest, considered the case of his son 'Nelly' and how he had shot another boy just for his props, his propeller wings, his rank with his peers. I studied and weighed the pros and cons of the case and found them all guilty.

Charles Jackson, his ex-partners, and that boy, guilty, the lot of them for the murder of Bennie Davies.

In that angry firelight, I realised that I too was heated, irritated by the fact that no one in that family saw any of this coming. I imagined Nelly's family, self-obsessed, co-dependent, chaotic, everyone fighting for their right to be seen in some type of narcissistic frenzy. The adults abandoning the children to their own devices, the children bonding together with other children, their frame of reference not from those adults charged to care for them, but from society. Abandoned by blood relations too bloody ignorant to see beyond themselves, the mirror of who they are probably sitting in their children's eyes.

Whilst the children not old enough to have any sense of who they are then turn to that uncaring parent, with an uncaring frame of reference, not willing, not equipped to care for its young.

"No wonder they get themselves into so much trouble," I whispered, as Hobo turned his head to me from nearby, perhaps thinking I was talking to him.

Yet, the person I was most pissed off about was the father, the man who had raised this child, or at least who had provided his sperm in a short frenzy of sweaty lovemaking then promptly fallen off the earth.

Charles Jackson. I resented him because he talked a good game, because he reminded me of all those other do-gooders out there who want the power and the kudos of saying the right thing whilst making a mess of their own lives.

"Talking down when fucking up," I said, smiling to myself.

He reminded me of so many of the men, the fathers, out there. The ones who want to be seen to say the right thing, but don't then do the right thing themselves.

"Like my own father."

Even though I had read the email from my mother, and even though I now felt a miniscule sense of sadness at his deterioration, I still felt critical of this man: this man who would abuse emotionally, physically, and sexually: this man who didn't care about the wounds he was inflicting on his wife and his son.

I remember the last time we talked about young black men, the last time we had any real type of conversation about anything remotely personal, about anything faintly deep.

It was Christmas Day just a couple of years ago. We were sitting on the sofa listening to some old jazz that I had bought him, and were talking about a number of things impacting on our society. It was a difficult conversation to have on the holiday, and all I wanted to do was relax and just enjoy those few days that I had free from the office.

Yet, my father, this man, kept bringing the conversation back to this point.

"What is wrong with black boys today?" he kept on saying. "They just seem so unruly, as if they have no sense."

He would criticise them, put them down, make out they were the worst of the low, before feeling some sense of generosity and adding that maybe economic factors had an impact on them: or maybe the racist environment they live in had an impact on them, things that were out of their control.

"But they are just so lazy and useless."

And the conversation would build and build, and I would hold back and hold back, knowing that this man liked to debate, that my father liked to create and argument.

As Dr Who played on television, I knew that this man was working himself up to a frenzy of frightening proportions, that should I engage him further we would argue, we would fight, and all the criticism of black men would land on me.

I would be lazy for not having the right job given my education: I would be stupid for not knowing the things that he knew: I would be worthless for not having a family or any children.

Yet, he would never acknowledge those black men who were more in life, the Barack Obama's of the world, or the Usain Bolt's: the Prince's of this world or the Kofi Annan's. He was a man who didn't want to see the many black people, the many black men, who had made it to become something more. From broken homes to solid ones: from abusive backgrounds to secure ones, he just didn't see it. And at no time did he ever take personal responsibility for the failures of his son.

Just like the narcissistic Charles Jackson he couldn't take responsibility for the fiasco of his own offspring. No. That would be to admit being a failure, and no narcissist can have that lest it shatter his already fragile sense of self into a thousand pointy, little, shards of glass.

No, they just distance themselves from whatever is happening. The pair of them, and many others from many cultures, would just remove themselves from the person they created, like an artist who paints a picture and blames its critical ridicule on an unfriendly press. The blame would always go outwards, like the pain, and like the learning experience that might have produced something better the next time.

Like Nelson 'Nelly' Jackson, who I supposed was still sitting in his prison cell, I didn't miss my father. I didn't regret leaving home after all those years of turmoil and abuse. I didn't feel any sadness towards that lost lonely man, sitting in his own world as his mind closed in around him.

I barely felt pity for him, and even that was gift from the gods.

I had learnt more about myself through sitting in that Dhow with Mudi these past few months than I ever had with my own father. I'd had more pleasant conversations with him as well, and felt in relation with, not talked down to. I had discussed subjects keen to both our hearts, and trusted him enough to open up about who I was and what I wanted from my life: parts of myself I would never trust my own father with.

Suddenly, Hobo barked, something he rarely did with such aggression, the force shocking me so that my head turned towards him. I watched as he just stood there, still growling softly, wary and watching something behind me.

"What is it boy?" I said in an attempt to calm him.

All he did though was bark again whilst taking a couple of hesitant steps forward.

I stopped, and considered myself, sensing a presence I had not felt for several months, before I turned towards it.

She was just stood there wearing one of her old gowns that I remembered from my childhood, looking only slightly older than when I last saw her. Her hair now had some whispers of grey in it that glinted in the firelight, grey that I had not seen before, and her skin looked as if it held more lines as well.

There were tears running down her cheeks, I could see, and her mouth held a hopeful half-smile, as if she couldn't really believe that it was me, whilst in her left hand she held a white scrunched up handkerchief.

"My son," was all she said to me, barely able to contain her emotions.

And right then I knew the endgame had begun.

Twenty

"What are you doing here?" I asked rising to my feet, trying but failing to withhold my anger from her.

My mother walked over to me, the tears still streaming free, and wiped her eyes with the handkerchief in her left hand, whilst with her right she reached up to caress my cheek.

Her hand felt coarse and grating on my face, but still I didn't push it away.

"What are you doing here?" I repeated.

But still she continued staring at me, as if needing to take me in totally, as if she were literally burning my image onto her mind's eye.

"You've lost weight," she replied in almost a whisper.

"You shouldn't be here," my words sharpened by my finally removing her now offensive hand from my face. "You should be with father, you should be back in London looking after him."

"I needed to find you."

"Well you managed it," I countered sharply. "Now go home and leave me alone."

Then, after calling Hobo to my side, I walked away leaving that woman, my mother, on a beach in Africa alone at night.

"You should not have left her like that," Mudi said the following morning as we sat down and had breakfast.

Mudi had just returned from his ablutions and wanted to hear about this woman who had arrived so late in the evening to find me. He told me about her urgency when she saw him in the hut, with her quickly spoken questions, and her joyous shaking of his hand when he had answered them.

I in turn told him what had happened during our brief meeting on the beach. I told him the things I couldn't tell her beyond the fact I didn't want to see her: that I didn't like her touching me, and that in some ways I hated her for what she had done to me.

Mudi though didn't like the conclusion.

"Nothing would have happened," I replied. "She is a game old woman, and has always been able to look after herself. And besides, I saw the driver she'd hired when I came back here. He would have taken her back to her hotel I'm sure."

Mudi disagreed. "That is not the point. She is an old woman. She has travelled all this way to talk to you. Now is the time. You two need to sit down and deal with this for once and for all."

"No," I said, shaking my head furiously, my fists clenched in anger. "I don't want her here, and I don't want to see her. I just want to be on my own, to work here with you, and to spend time with Hobo."

My elderly friend just looked at me. "I know you didn't sleep that well. You know within you that there is something you have to unravel, so go and do it. I am not going to be taking you out in the boat today, I can fish on my own whilst you talk to your mother."

"What?"

"Don't argue with me. She is your mother, and here in Africa we respect them as much as we respect our fathers. You may think you don't like her, but she has such an impact on you. I have seen how moody you are when you read your emails from home, and know how long it takes you to recover yourself from those moods, to return to the young man I've come to know so well, but you can't go on like this. It isn't natural."

"I don't want to talk to her," I replied, sounding very much like a petulant boy in an argument with his father.

"Yes you do. She told me this might happen, so she told me that she will be on the beach by the hotel in the village this morning. Go and see her there, sort this out, and find yourself again. You owe yourself that much, and me too."

I looked at him. Mudi's face was set in a painful smile, as if what he was asking me to do was literally tearing at his heart.

I couldn't turn him down, I found. I couldn't let down this man who had taken me in, who had fed me and treated me almost like his own son.

"You win," I said finally.

We watched as a herd of emaciated cows drifted along the beach towards us with their calves, skinny things all of them with thin tails in constant movement as they waved the numerous flies away.

My mother and myself watched them as they passed us, the only creatures other than us on this stretch of beach. I turned to gaze out at the turquoise sea as it crept ever closer in its consistent rolling motion.

There I was, I thought to myself. There I was with my mother, just the pair of us on this deserted patch of paradise, walking side by side like lovers.

"Why are you here?" I asked finally, having done the small talk. My mother had told me just how things were back in Britain, with its financial crisis, the banks going under, and the early days of the new President of the United States of America.

We had talked our way through all of the meaningless things that helped us to build some type of connection: like a rickety wooden bridge over a vast and deep ravine.

"Why do you think?" she replied. "Because I needed to see you."

"Well you have seen me now mother. You can see I'm well, so you don't need to stay, you can go home now."

She stopped there right then, as if frozen, as if wanting to say something more, but struggling to find the words, whilst I just continued my amble along that beach.

"Karl."

I turned as she whispered my name, a name she rarely actually used.

"I miss you so much."

"What?"

"I miss you," she repeated, walking up towards me. Again she placed that palm on my face. This time I immediately brushed it away.

"Why did you leave me?"

"Because I've always been there for you," I replied hesitantly. "Because I was always the one who had to save you, and when the abuse finally came out, it all hit me really hard, but you didn't care."

Her questioning eyes held their sadness as she looked at me. "I don't understand."

I glared at her. “No, you probably don’t. Do you really think I didn’t know what was going on under the surface? Do you not realise how scared I was of that man when I was younger, or know how unhappy you both were? I saw it mother, I saw it and felt it. Day after day, I lived through it.

“Do you remember those times when I was a child when father used to hit you? Those times when I was just too young to do anything about it, too young to stand up to father, when I had barely even begun school?”

“Yes.”

“Then you also remember how you used to hide behind me. How when father came at you in one of his rages you used to you used to race into the bedroom to find me and cuddle me, as if I was your human shield, as if I was your saviour.”

“Yes,” she replied, her head bowing guiltily at the memory.

“How do you think that made me feel?”

“I don’t know.”

“I was terrified mother. I was so scared that I didn’t know what to do, so I just clung to you. Like a child should do, I just hung onto you.”

“I know.”

“And what did you do?”

I watched as my mother lowered her head. “I don’t remember,” she replied.

“When I needed you most, when I needed to feel safe, you know what you did? You used to brush me off you. When you felt better, safer in the world, you used to push me away from you and go about your business. So that when I still needed someone, when I needed to feel cared for you weren’t there for me. Yet, I always was for you.”

“I don’t remember any of that. I didn’t know that was how you felt.”

“And why should you?” I continued. “Why should you know anything about me, or about how I felt back then? You didn’t care for me. That whole situation wasn’t about my feeling safe. It was about you feeling loved, and safe, and connected. I was that protector mother; your saviour, your lover, your friend. You were never mine.”

"But I was there for you, I must have been, you must understand that. I fed you and clothed you, took you to school and sent you on holidays. I prayed to God so much to keep you safe…"

"Yet not once, not once, did you ever tell me you loved me. Not once did you ever say to me that you cared. Do you know where I learnt to love myself mother, where I learned that I was respected and cared for?"

I waited in silence whilst she shook her head.

"In those comic books I used to read. All those dreams I used to have of being a hero, of saving the world. I used to live out that same fantasy in my imagination that I did in real life, yet this time I was loved for it. This time I got the hugs, the kisses, the sex. This time I got the girl.

"But you know one thing I didn't do back when father was abusing us? The one thing I would never allow myself to express in front of you?"

"No."

"I would never cry."

I watched as my mother raised her head to look at me, a nameless look in her eyes, as if she didn't quite understand what I meant.

So I continued. "I didn't cry because, like all those heroes I used to pretend to be, I had learnt to be strong for you. I'd learnt that I had to hold myself together and be there for you. That no matter how scared I was for and of you, I needed to hold myself together for long enough to keep you safe. I had learnt, even then, that I was there to protect you."

I just stood there as my mother looked at me, not adding anything more, not even attempting to sugar the words I had used, hoping that a few of them had hit home.

"I had no idea you were so angry with me," she said finally.

"Yes I am," I replied calmly. "I'm absolutely furious with you."

"You don't have that right," she whispered on hearing me admit my rage with her.

"What?"

"You don't have the right to be angry with me," she repeated, this time with more volume.

"You have got to be joking."

"You don't have the right to be angry with me. I'm your mother!" Now she was finding her voice. Now she was rising to meet me in my challenge.

"Tell me why not?"

"I've just told you. I brought you into this world, I made you, I gave birth to you. We don't do anger at mothers in our culture. I couldn't be angry with my mother, and she couldn't be angry with hers. It wasn't allowed then, as it has always been, so you don't have the right to be angry at me."

"But you used me!" I shouted, shocking her.

"What?"

"You used me for your own ends. You used me to feel loved, so that I would only express nice feelings towards you. No sadness, no pain, no loneliness, and definitely no shame. I had to be your emotionless protector, and had no right to express the one emotion every child needs to. His anger, and especially at his parents, and especially at his mother."

"I don't know what to say…" she stumbled in reply.

"Then maybe I should continue. Do you understand just how many times I've dropped what I was doing and run to your door, to your aid, to see if you were alright? Letting go of what might have been important for me to save you, to help you, to be there for someone who used to push me away like a soiled toiletry."

I turned towards the rolling waves as she just stared at me and we stood there silent, the time passing, slowly, painfully.

"You were always there for me," she admitted, her confession calming me.

I found myself attracted by the sound of birds gliding on the breeze over the sea. "Yes I was. So please understand the reasons for my being out here, the reason I had to leave. I needed to find myself."

"What do you mean?"

"I needed to know who I am, mum? I had to start to discover who am I other than Superboy, your Friendly Neighbourhood Rescuer? Who am I really underneath that cloak you created for me?" As I talked I mimicked a superhero, taking flight, spraying webs, punching out a bad guy.

"Don't be so silly!" mother chided, folding her arms.

I stopped and stared at her once more. "Alright, then why don't you tell me something about me? Can you do that?"

"Of course," she replied. "I'm your mother. Of course I know all about you."

"Then tell me something intimate about me. Don't bother telling me about Lilly, or work, as those are things that everyone knows. Let's see if you can tell me something different. Go on mum, tell me about me."

And even though I had pushed her into this position, even though I knew what the answer would be, I was still surprised by just how badly my mother stumbled over her answer. I was shocked by how difficult it was to tell me something about me.

"You're right, I don't know that much about you."

"Exactly," I replied, angry again. "Because my life has always been about you. My whole existence from a boy to a man has been about keeping you safe, about holding your fear, mirroring your self: not about being there for me, about teaching me all that I should know to feel safe in the world. Do you know why it took me so long to leave home? Because I was scared mother, because I was frightened of what I might find out there, and because I was terrified of what I might leave behind. And do you know why I've never had a decent relationship mother?"

"You had Lilly," she interrupted, finding a little voice under my tirade. "She was a good woman before she found God. You should have stayed with her."

"I always had other women on the side, mother," I countered. "I was sleeping with another woman from time to time, someone who I could just fuck when I felt like it. Blimey, that shows just how much you don't know about me. I didn't want to commit fully to any woman because I was scared, because I was worried I might become the same person dad was, or end up in the same position I was in with you: consumed by your need to feel safe.

"And do you know what else all this cost me? It cost me myself. It cost me knowing who I am, it cost me any type of relationship with my father, and any type of healthy one with my mother. It cost me courtships, friendships, my anger, and my drive and determination to be something more in life. I'm a broken man mother. Just see how your relationship has now left me."

I was standing there shaking, but could now see the beginning of tears forming in my mother's eyes.

"But don't you see what your father has done?" she pleaded. "He is the one wholly at fault here. He is the one who abused us both, who beat me and undermined you. Your father, that man, is the one who used to spit on me for no reason. He is the one who beat me when I was pregnant with you. He is the one who left my face so bruised at times that I couldn't leave the house for days. So, HE is the one you should be angry at, not me."

"Oh, don't push all of that onto him," I countered. "Yes, he is guilty, he has always been guilty, but this is what we do. We take mother and make her good, then take father and make him bad, but it's not as simple as that. You both have a role to play in this, and for making the life of your only son such a nightmare.

"I walked on eggshells around him for years, not wanting to do anything, anything at all to upset him. I didn't want to make him angry, to make him sad, or even to make him happy, because I knew none of this would last and he would revert to type. But you know what? I always knew when you were upset too. There were times when I would feel the need to call you before you even knew it yourself. There were times when I could tell from the look on your face, or from a gesture of your hand just how low you were inside. And during those times, I always felt guilty because there was nothing I could do to help you."

And right then, I could feel the tears forming in my eyes as that same guilt rose up from deep within me once more: that first feeling, that sense conceived in my senses when I was still in the womb, that wound I would always carry with me.

I wanted this to be over, but still I had more to say. I needed to prove my point, to make her understand me, to make her see me for the first time in our lives together.

Then surprisingly, as she stood there staring at me, watching me emote before her, she did just that.

"I had no idea that it would affect you so," she said softly. "I really didn't think about just how much having a man like that or a woman like myself in the house would impact you. They say so much about children being resilient, about kids sometimes being able to cope better than adults, but maybe that is because they absorb so much of what goes on around them, and if it's bad they hide it away, storing it for a time when they might be able to discharge it somewhere. Only, they forget, or there is nowhere else to go, so they end up carrying it around forever like you. Oh my son, what have I done to you? I'm so very sorry. I'm so sorry Karl."

Suddenly thankful, I sighed, noting that my shoulders were still sagging with the weight of the guilt placed upon them. "Now do you see why I had to leave?"

Mother nodded at me, but I still felt the need to continue.

"I left because I wanted to experience me away from all of that chaos at home. I wanted to feel free for the first time in ages. And do you know what happened when I began all this, when I came here on holiday? I went and joined a group of people who were just as frightened as myself, and therefore just as reluctant to fully engage in the world as me."

"Kerry told me," mother added, nodding her head. "I spoke to her when I was trying to find you. She said she understood your search: that you needed to just be on your own, and that she saw the fear in you when you were at the orphanage. I didn't realise it was that way within you."

"Yet, even when I worked in Dar Es Salaam I still found myself falling for someone I could rescue."

"You mean Mary?"

"Yes. She was no different to all the other women I've met over the years, mother. She was just the same as Lilly, and just the same as you, and I hated myself when I realised what type of woman I had found myself attracted to once again."

"So that is why you had to leave there so quickly."

"Yes. I just needed to free myself from all that fear for once and for all."

As the sea began its retreat, and the wind turned, she just looked at me, my mother. Her brow furrowed, her greying hair blowing in the wind she studied me, maybe for the first time since I was born, as if trying to see me, trying to understand just who I was, or who I had become.

We walked a little further, my mother ahead of me, her head bowed as if deep in thought. "And what about your life here? What has that brought you?"

"I'm happy here, mother," I started to reply. "For all I've been through, this is the first time I can honestly say that, and it's bliss. I don't want to lose that. Not for you or for anyone."

She nodded to me, perhaps finally fully realising the full extent of just how far I had come on this journey. "And Mudi?"

"Well, what can I say?" I replied with a shrug. "He has been good to me like no other man has before. He took me in, showed me kindness, and has even taught me a trade, even though I doubt fishing is something I could ever use in London."

We both chuckled at that, finally finding something amusing within all of this.

"But you have to understand, Mudi has been like a father to me. It hasn't been easy for me, mum. I'm not used to walking around someone, a man even, with so much ease and lightness. I'm not used to having a man encourage me to do well and praising me when I do. I'm not used to a man teaching me how I should be out in the world. It was him who encouraged me to come and meet you today, and I still only did so because I admire and respect him. The only reason I would do something similar for father would be because I was afraid of him, not because I cared about what he had to say."

"I can see that in him," mother said calmly. "He is a good man. I could feel that from the moment when I first met him. When I found him, and told him why I was there, he didn't say much to me, he just nodded his head and told me that he understood. The one thing that did strike me was how gentle yet strong he seemed. I haven't seen a man like that for many years. Maybe not since my grandfather."

"Then you get why I feel so safe here."

Mother stopped and nodded her head at me.

"But you still want me to come home? I know you do, I can still feel you."

Again, she started to cry. This woman, my mother, her eyes squeezing free drops of moisture, her emotions radiating a sense of her sadness without her son, or maybe her marriage.

"You know me so well," she said softly.

"Yes I do," I replied coldly. "And that is the problem."

Twenty-One

Mudi cooked for us later that evening, saving three large red crabs from his daily catch for us to have with some rice.

It was dusk by the time we returned from our walk, my mother and myself, and as we walked up the beach towards the small village we saw Mudi there, with the fire starting to glow red in its pit in the sand.

Taking a few seconds to greet us, he then went back to preparing our evening meal, whilst Hobo drifted back from wherever he had been, looking sorry and rejected as if he hadn't received enough attention that day.

"Silly thing," I said to him, kneeling down so I could stroke his coat roughly and send his tail wagging.

Mother watched all of this going on, and I could sense her feeling taken aback by the richness of the simple fare, a meal made by the hand of this gentle kind man, and the contented happiness of the three of us, man, boy and dog.

As the food was served she sat beside the fire, before wrapping a long blue shawl around her shoulders which Mudi had brought out from the hut for her.

"Your father never lifted a finger to help in the kitchen," she reminded me as she thanked Mudi, before eagerly cracking a crab claw. "Not even at Christmas."

"I remember that, but I also recall you regularly complaining that I wouldn't help either, then shooing me away when I offered. It was like I couldn't win."

Mother smiled to herself at that, and thought for a minute. "You are right, I did used to do that. Maybe I was more controlling than I realised back when you were young."

"What was Karl like?" asked Mudi, a mischievous look in his eye. As I glanced at him, I could see he was attempting to shift the conversation away from anything maudlin. He just gave me his now familiar wink to let me know that I was in trouble.

"Well, he was a good boy on the whole," mother replied, a look of pride suddenly coming to her face.

"What do you mean on the whole?" Mudi probed, sensing something.

"Well, he was very untidy most of the time. There were always toys and clothes lying around his room, and he was continually in trouble at junior school for chatting too much in class. And then he was always playing silly games with his toys, creating worlds or something, but I would always hear him discussing things with his toy soldiers and the like. It was rather cute really."

"I was not," I snorted, feeling a little nervous.

Mudi meanwhile was busy laughing at me. "He talks a lot here too. You should see how he is with his silly dog. Always talking to it like it's a real person. Sometimes, I wonder if he imagines it answers back to him."

Hobo's ears seemed to perk up at this, and from where he was contentedly lying beside me he raised his head and yawned before staring at me.

"Don't worry, my friend," I said to him as I playfully scratched his nose. "They're just being mean about us. You know I can understand you fully, don't you."

Mother and Mudi both chuckled at the sight of her son, his friend, the man who could talk to animals, before the conversation moved on to other subjects, only occasionally settling on me and my childhood shenanigans.

As we ate and talked that night, I could feel a sense of ease build around that fire, as we relaxed, a difficult day over for us all. I could see the tension ease form my mother for the first time since we had rediscovered each other, as if she were finally enjoying the beauty of the scene, and her proximity to her son. I could see Mudi enjoying telling his stories to a crowd, like he always did, taking pleasure in the lightness he brought to all our eyes and faces. I could feel myself feeling vindicated for making the choices I had made these past nine months: that leaving my mother and father to find myself changed something for us all.

The next morning, mother came to the beach early at the turn of the tide to see us off to work out. Like a concerned mother maybe should, she stood there, her hands in the pockets of the skirt she wore that day, her face a mask of worry, as if mentally fussing about if her son would return from his day out in the oh-so-deadly seas off Tanzania.

I smiled as I left her, kissed her on the cheek, and went on my way, helping Mudi push the Dhow away from the shore yet again. I didn't mind that she saw me like this, my mother, in fact it pleased me that our roles were now obviously reversed like this, that I felt free enough to do this, and that she so worried about me when I did.

And for some reason I found myself working harder because of it. I discovered reserves of resilience within me that meant when I would normally want to stop for a break I would just keep on going.

Mudi, through his watchful gaze, chose not to comment on any difference, his eyes narrowing as I saw them occasionally alight on me.

I was still happy. I was still eager and content enough with my life that I wanted to stay here forever, that I was now free to do so, was now released from my prison as my mother's saviour. Now I could be me, I wanted to enjoy myself, I wanted to build a life here, to learn more Swahili, to get married, to have children and have Mudi be the 'Grandfather' to them that I so know he could be.

I truly wanted this to last forever.

The day before mother left was a Sunday, so Mudi took the boat out alone again, giving us both some time to enjoy the other's company one last time.

We didn't walk along the beach, instead choosing to sit by the sea and watch the women with their children as they played, danced, and sang songs together. The scene reminded me so much of when I was at the orphanage, the feelings of calm joy rising up within me yet again.

As they noticed us, they waved, encouraging us to come closer, so we did, sitting by the group and joining in.

"How do you know them?" mother asked me.

I smiled to myself at the recollection. "On the evening Obama was elected President of the United States, there was a big party out here, and Mudi and myself brought some fish for the villagers. Some of the men brought their drums and they needed another person to play, so they asked me. They know me from that night."

Mother looked at me, more than a little surprised. "You played the drums?"

"I don't that often, but I am learning. I actually enjoy it, and that night was one hell of a party, I can tell you. Everyone here is so proud of Obama, so proud of a black man making it as the President of America. There were many tears that night, mine included."

"Yes, I watched him speak on television. He did so very well."

We again lapsed into silence, my mother and I, continuing to listen to the sounds of the singing children, and the rhythm of the clapping mothers.

As I watched though, I felt as a sense of sadness that was alien to me, realising it was because of the proximity of my mother. A sense of anger, and of envy that I had never had these types of experiences then rose, that I had never felt this same ease that these children and their mothers feel around each other. I envied these children their gift, their unknown unconscious inheritance from the generation of loving mothers who were children before them.

I found myself beginning to resent those songs sang so sweetly, and the games played so freely, until I glanced at my mother and noticed the sadness and shame in her eyes, realising that she felt much the same as me. I imagined her feelings were in opposition to the mothers across from us, and pictured her wishing she could have been as comfortable enough within herself to have crawled down onto her knees and played with my toy soldiers with me.

I envisaged her sadness as one for those times seen and lost, those moments measured and discarded. Of those times when she might well have wanted to be down there with me, to give me another voice to talk to instead of my own, but was too afraid to get too close, to be there for me.

Or maybe she just simply didn't know how.

I didn't feel any guilt this time for her as I sat there. Instead, I felt a considerable compassion for this woman, my mother, who was next to me. All that sadness and compassion that we didn't have the relationship either of us deserved because of our personal inadequacies, or of our cultural inheritance: I didn't know or care which.

Eventually though she rose from the sand, before she brushed her skirt down, her emotions now hidden as she smiled at me.

"I'm hungry," she said calmly, as if nothing that I felt from her could have been real. "Let's get something to eat."

The following morning, I hired a car to take my mother back to the airport in Dar Es Salaam. On the way, I got around paying a couple of persistent policemen by showing them my British passport, encouraging them to think at the very least that I was just a tourist.

When we were stopped at a third checkpoint the policeman on duty scratched his head as if he recognised me, before saying a few words in Swahili that I failed to understand.

"I'm sorry, I don't know what you mean," I replied calmly.

The policeman looked at me quizzically, before pushing his head further into the car. Then he spotted my mother seated next to me, a calm measured look on her face, as if she were truly regal.

Promptly, he then gathered himself, as if recognising that he needed to respect this woman, before tapping the car door and waving me on.

"I should travel with you more often," I said to her as we drove away.

"I am glad you came."

We were at the airport outside Dar Es Salaam and mother had checked in for her flight back to London. Sitting on a couple of chairs before she entered the departure lounge, we had barely shared a word until then, until I had spoken, the atmosphere sad but not at all negative.

Mother looked at me, a small smile on her lips. "I'm glad I came as well," she replied, patting me lightly on the hand. "Your father will be happy that I've found you."

"Will he?"

"Of course. He does care for you, even though he may not say so."

I couldn't contain a snort of derision at the thought of my father caring. "Sometimes I find that hard to believe."

"I know you do, and I do as well sometimes, but he does care. I just don't think he feels he has the right to express that he does. Maybe that is his cultural legacy."

"Well, send him my best wishes. I don't wish him any harm."

Right then, a female voice called out my mother's flight, so we both rose, knowing full well that this was it, that this was the end of our time together. I manoeuvred her bags out of the way so there was just the two of us, just me and her, my mother, that woman, facing each other and about to say goodbye.

And for only the second time since she had found me I felt some compassion for this sad, lonely, destroyed old woman. As I looked into her eyes I realised just how lonely she was, and felt the guilt that would in the past have pulled me back to her side, abandoning myself, leaving myself as lonely as she was. So, for both our sakes, I contained it, I held onto those feelings and just hugged her. I held my mother tight in an intimate embrace and told her I loved her, before she whispered the same to me and started to cry once again.

"Keep in touch," she continued. "You need to send your mother an email occasionally. You're useless at keeping in touch."

"I know," I replied smiling. "I promise to do better this time. I promise to write emails of my own."

"And don't forget I love you," she added.

Then with a final soft smile I let go, giving her the bags, and guided her through to the Immigration Desk on the first leg of her journey home.

"Bail out the boat boy!"

Even though my arms ached from the repeated exertion of hoisting water out of our dhow with that little plastic bottle cut in two, I still smiled at Mudi. He was sat across from me, his eyes scanning the horizon, watching as a brace of black clouds rolled slowly in towards us.

"Will we make it before the storm hits?"

Mudi raised a hand to shield his eyes. “We should be fine,” he replied. “But we won’t make it if you don’t keep doing what you’re supposed to.”

I couldn’t help but smile at that. “I’m doing my best. Sometime soon we really must get a proper bucket for this boat.”

“They’re too expensive.”

“I have some money still in my account. I could buy one for us both.”

“Hmm,” Mudi mused. “I don’t think so.”

“”Why not?” I asked, already knowing the answer.

“Because then it will be easier for you. This is good work, hard work, and it gives you something useful to do.”

I couldn’t help but laugh at him. I already knew that Mudi liked it when I bailed out the boat. It gave him something to complain about, and allowed him to boss me around. Whilst in turn I allowed him his pleasure, as he taught me my trade, as he gave me the skills to be the man I needed to be.

It had been a month since my mother had left Tanzania by now, and although I missed her at times I felt happy that I was finally able to strike out on my own. I still worked the days with Mudi, still fed our dog Hobo, and had even been spending time with a young woman from the village from the night of Obama’s victory.

I was building a life here for myself now, away from the chaos of Dar and of London. Separate from the abuse of my parents, and of my position as their referee, their saviour. I was free of the fear that kept me in that cultural bubble back in Zambia, and happier than I had been in the Miami Bar in Dar.

I was putting on weight, becoming more muscular, more substantial, more defined. There was more to me in what I ate, what I did, and how I was with others. I had learnt to dance, played the drums and even went out fishing on my own.

And as I mused over all the changes that had occurred to me since that last final meeting on the beaches here in the south of Tanzania, I found myself smiling about how lucky I was that such a difficult beginning could bring itself to so brilliant a conclusion. I was lucky, this was a good life separate from others, but still engaged.

"The water boy, bail it out!" shouted Mudi as he pulled at the sail once more.

Yes, this was a good life. Good enough.

Printed in Great Britain
by Amazon

57910873R00122